MW00944037

Annie
Blue-Eyes

Annie Blue-Eyes

Copyright © 2014 Lynne Gardner Cook

ALL RIGHTS RESERVED

No part of this book may be reproduced or transmitted in any form or by any means, electronic or mechanical, including photocopying, recording, or by any information storage or retrieval system, without prior written permission from the copyright owner unless such copying is expressly permitted by federal copyright law. The publisher is not authorized to grant permission for further uses of copyrighted selections printed in this book. Permission must be obtained from the individual copyright owners identified herein. Requests for permission should be addressed to the publisher.

Published by Line by Lion, LLC, 2025 Bell Rd.
Morgantown, IN 46160

Cover art by Zak Kendall

ISBN 978-1-940938-35-6

This is a work of fiction. Names, characters, places and incidents are products of the author's imagination or are used for literary purpose and are not to be construed as real. Any resemblance to actual events, locales, organizations, or persons, living or dead, are entirely coincidental. The names of actual locations and products are used solely for literary effect and should neither be taken as endorsement nor as a challenge to any associated trademarks.

Annie
Blue-Eyes

Lynne Gardner Cook

Prologue

Annie crouched in the woods watching helplessly as her best (and only) friend spun away from her, out into the dark, circling water. How was she going to save him? She was just a small mouse, and the water was so deep. Even if she could save him, where would they go from here? They had no idea how to get out of this huge forest.

How had she come to be in this predicament? Oh, she knew the answer to that question! It was clearly the fault of that wretched boy, Raymond Ratchet. It'd all started when he took her away from her family and her beloved home in the pet store. It'd all gone downhill from there; just one trying circumstance after another. She'd suffered everything from near starvation to near extinction!

How many times had she barely escaped with her life from how many horrors?

Annie couldn't even count them, but none

of this was going to stop her from her mission to find her true home. As soon as she managed this rescue, they were going to press on and find their way out of this dangerous place. Annie was determined to find out where she really belonged.

SEVERAL WEEKS EARLIER . . . .

Chapter One

The Pet Store

"Oh, no!" Annie whispered to her younger brother. "I hope that noisy boy isn't coming over here!"

Annie and Barry watched from the safety of their glass house in Mr. Dailey's pet shop, as Raymond Ratchet came banging through the store's front door. He looked back over his shoulder at his mother, demanding loudly, "You said I could have a pet, and I want one now."

His mother sighed. "Well, nothing too big. And remember, no reptiles!"

"Fine!" Raymond retorted. He ranged up and down the aisles of the pet store, glaring into one display case after another. He muttered to himself, "It doesn't have to be big, it just has to be cool!"

Raymond looked wistfully into the tanks containing snakes and lizards, but he knew his mother wouldn't budge on that one. Her fear of reptiles was something that could not be surmounted. He skipped swiftly past the tanks of colorful tropical fish. You couldn't do anything with a fish. And he didn't even let himself look at the dogs. There was no way his mom would let him have a dog. They definitely fit into the category of "too big."

Finally, Raymond entered the rodent aisle. Annie watched fretfully as he came closer. She was the oldest of the mouse siblings, followed by Barry, Carrie, Danny and Ethel. She looked like all her brothers and sisters, with sleek, white fur, tiny, pinkish paws, and a long, furless tail. In fact, she looked just like every other white mouse, except for the fact that, instead of having red eyes, hers were a bright and true blue.

When Mr. Dailey had first seen Annie open those blue eyes, he'd known she was special. Mr. Dailey cared about all the pets in his store, but he knew that he particularly would not look forward to selling such an unusual mouse. However, he realized that the time would arrive when a prospective pet-owner would come along, and Mr. Dailey couldn't expect any of his mice to stay in their crowded pet-store homes when the opportunity to live with a human family presented itself.

As Raymond approached the mouse family's glass case, Annie's heart pounded. "Barry, we have to get out of here!" she squealed, jumping onto their exercise wheel.

"Annie, you know you won't actually go anywhere in that thing," Barry reminded her with a brotherly chuckle.

"I know . . . I know!" Annie panted. "I just feel like I have to get away from that boy. I have to MOVE!" she added, as she spun the wheel as fast as her tiny feet could go.

The boy stopped short right in front of the mouse family's glass home. He took one look at Annie with her unlikely blue eyes and knew this was the pet for him. Raymond was ten years old. He was thin, and tall for his age — all angles and elbows. He had stringy, reddish hair, which he kept out of his way by swiping at it frequently with his freckled fingers. By the time Mr. Dailey joined him in the rodent aisle, Raymond had already named this marvelous mouse. He'd seen how fast Annie could make her little wheel spin, and he'd made the decision on the spot to name her "Super Speed King." (Raymond didn't know she was a girl.)

When Mrs. Ratchet expressed her doubts about having a rodent in the house, Raymond was extremely persuasive. "Come on, Mom," he whined. "He's not a reptile, and you said nothing too big. You can't get much smaller than a mouse. And I'll feed him and take care of him, and it'll be really cool!"

Mrs. Ratchet finally relented, and, despite his fondness for Annie, Mr. Dailey agreed to sell the little blue-eyed mouse. Soon, Annie was bidding a tearful goodbye to her parents and brothers and sisters as Mr. Dailey gently handed her into a small cardboard box.

"No, Mama, no!" she wailed, scratching at the sides of the box. Annie wondered how her parents could let her go, as Raymond marched triumphantly out of the store, box and mouse in hand.

Raymond took Annie home and set up a little house for her in an old fish tank in his bedroom. He filled it with good-smelling pine shavings and a shiny new racing wheel. She had a little feeding bowl filled with all sorts of seeds, and a hanging bottle for drinking water.

Annie began to think that having a human family might be almost as good as being with her mouse family. Raymond thought Annie was the most wonderful and fascinating thing in the world, and he took very fine care of her — for about a week.

Raymond soon became more interested in a new video game his friend Zach had loaned him. Then it was a fighter plane model, which got left in a half-finished gluey heap on his dresser. From then on, Raymond would only feed Annie when his mother yelled at him about "cruelty to animals" and "common decency." Pretty soon, Annie was all out of food and almost out of water, but not out of hope!

Chapter Two

The Escape

Annie was not one to languish during trying times. She'd been forced to develop a sense of independence since she'd been abandoned by her family and by her new owner. This little mouse had spent many a long day and night with no one to play with and no one to talk to but herself. Now she'd have to demonstrate that she could be quite resourceful, also. When it became apparent that she was definitely on her own in the food and beverage department, Annie knew that she had to get out of that tank.

"I don't need anyone to help me," she declared. "If Mr. Dailey and my parents don't want me, I don't want them, either! If Raymond isn't interested in me, then I don't care about him. I can take care of myself, and I can figure out a way to escape all by myself, too," she thought.

Annie pressed her nose against the cool glass of the fish tank, staring out into Raymond's bedroom in search of an idea that could aid her quest for freedom. As her blue eyes scanned the messy room, they lit on Raymond's sweatshirt in a wrinkled heap on the floor. She thought back to several days before. The boy had carelessly tossed his sweatshirt onto the fish tank as he'd hurried through the room, and its sleeve had dangled down into the pine chips. At the time, Annie had thought about how she could so easily have skittered up that sleeve and climbed right out of the tank. But why would she, since she had everything she needed right there? Hah! If she'd only known then how temporary her easy life would be.

"Okay, fine," Annie said to herself, closing her eyes to concentrate on formulating an escape plan. "What I know now is that I need to get out of here. I just need Raymond to come in here and throw his sweatshirt (or something) up here onto the tank again. If he'd just. . . ." Annie's musings were interrupted by an ear-splitting sound.

MMMMrrreeeeooooow! Annie's eyes flew open to behold a terrifying sight. Glaring directly at her were two huge, yellow eyes, belonging to a large black cat. As Annie stared in frozen horror, the cat pressed his pink nose against the glass, letting out a low, menacing growl. Annie's mind raced. Was the glass wall of the fish tank secure enough to protect her from this horrifying creature? Perhaps not. As Annie watched in helpless fright, the cat's leering grin inched slowly up the glass. Before the little mouse knew what was happening, the lithe feline had leaped to the upper edge of the tank and thrust his paw, with claws extended, down toward Annie's terror-stricken face.

Annie pressed herself down into the pine chips as far as she could, but she quickly realized that, if the cat elected to jump down into the tank with her, she wouldn't stand a chance of escape. She watched, transfixed, as the clawed paw swiped the air just over her head again and again. "Come on — think!" Annie commanded herself. As she helplessly watched the cat's deadly attempts to reach her, her little rodent life flashed before her eyes. Beginning with that moment and moving quickly backwards, her mouse memories raced through her head and came to an abrupt halt on that scene from the previous week — the sweatshirt hanging over the edge of the tank. As she watched the cat's thick black tail dangling down into the tank, a risky plan began to form. Could she possibly grab that tail and climb to freedom before the cat's deadly jaws could snatch her up?

As the next claw-swipe came dangerously close to her quivering whiskers, Annie knew that she had to act now or never. She jumped up, ran along the base of the glass as fast as she could, and gave a mighty leap upward just as the sinewy tale came flicking down toward her. The little mouse latched on with all four paws and several teeth. The cat let out a surprised yowl and snapped his tail straight up. Acting on pure instinct, Annie let go of the tail and found herself sailing through the air. She shot in a high arc up toward Raymond's toy shelf, and flew directly into the tummy of a fluffy old teddy bear.

Clinging to the furry fellow for a few moments, Annie caught her breath and looked out over the bedroom from her new vantage point. The first thing she noticed was the extremely annoyed cat, hissing and snapping his head from side to side. Annie watched in fascination as her would-be captor slunk all over the room, looking under the bed and behind the desk in search of his recent prey, knocking over books and toys along the way.

Before the confused cat could notice Annie on the toy shelf above him, both cat and mouse were startled by the sound of footsteps coming up the stairs.

Mrs. Ratchet came stalking into the room,

demanding "What is all this racket? Oh, you again!" she accused, snatching the cat up in her hands. Holding the twisting feline at arm's length and stomping back down the stairs, Mrs. Ratchet could be heard railing at the cat.

"I can't believe you snuck into our house again, Lucifer! Why can't you stay in your own house? Did Raymond leave the door open again? Why. . . ." Her voice trailed off, and Annie breathed a huge sigh of relief, as she heard the front door slam.

"I did it! I'm free!" the little mouse realized. Although she'd had no opportunity to use it before, Annie soon discovered her ability as a mouse to jump impressive distances. Without even thinking about it first, she leaped from the shelf to the desk to the floor — easy as pie. "Wow! That was awesome!" she exulted.

Even stronger than her instinct for jumping was Annie's instinct for finding food. She scampered about Raymond's room, looking for something — anything — to eat. How wonderful it felt to know that she could run as far and as fast as she wanted! Annie followed her nose, and it led her to the shadowy and rather smelly region under Raymond's bed. There, Annie found plates and cups and bowls filled with all kinds of tasty tidbits. After consuming part of a glazed donut, several bites of a chocolate-chip cookie, and two raisins, she was more than full. Now well-fueled for further adventure, Annie began a thorough investigation of her new home, which spread out around her in every direction.

Chapter Three

The Ice Cream

Later that afternoon, Annie's explorations were interrupted by the sound of Raymond's strident voice coming down the hallway as he spoke to his friend Zach. Like Raymond, Zach was also ten years old. He was just a bit pudgy, in a puppy sort of way, and he had a bristly crew-cut of dark brown hair.

"Why do you want to see that mouse again, Zach? I think he's pretty lame, but you can — Hey! Where is he?"

Annie sat bolt upright. She couldn't let that boy find her and put her back in the tank! She sprang off the baseball glove she'd been investigating and zigzagged between all the clothes, kitchenware, and toys under Raymond's bed until she reached the wall. She pressed herself against the baseboard as Raymond knelt down and peered into the shadows beneath his bed. He began thrashing his arm back and forth through all the junk, saying, "I'll bet he's under here. When I find you, you little rat. . . ."

Annie had nearly given up all hope of keeping her new-found freedom, when the shrill sound of a bell came clearly through the open window.

"Ice cream man!" cried Zach.

"Ow!" yelped Raymond, as he banged his head on the bottom edge of the bed frame.

"Come on. Let's go, Ray!" Zach caroled, and they were off and running, not another thought given to the tiny escapee.

Although it was clear, despite the abundant food supply, that Raymond's bedroom was not a safe place for her to stay, Annie found herself too frightened to move out from under the bed. On paws that were still a bit shaky, she finally crept back to the baseball glove, and made a mad dash across the room to the open door.

Annie poked her nose around the corner of the doorway, sniffing cautiously. When no dangerous-smelling scents met her nostrils, she followed with her whiskers and her bright blue eyes. Since there was no one in the hallway, Annie skittered along the hall wall until she came to a carpeted staircase. The steps looked pretty steep, but the brave little mouse found that she could climb down backwards, one step at a time, if she went slowly and carefully and didn't think too much about what might be at the bottom. Nine steps . . . Ten . . . eleven. She made it!

Annie looked around quickly and saw that she was still alone. She scooted across the empty downstairs hallway and came to the entrance of a room that was bigger than Raymond's bedroom. Immediately to her right, she spied a large piece of upholstered furniture, which sat low to the ground. By creeping along under its scalloped, fabric edge, Annie could observe the whole room.

At right angles to the piece of furniture under which she hid, was another, smaller couch of the same fabric, and on it sat Raymond and Zach, loudly slurping and licking at drippy double-decker ice cream cones. Annie shot back toward the wall, under cover of the larger couch. Before she could think of what to do next, she heard Raymond's mother come into the room.

"How many times have I told you not to eat in the living room? Now take that ice cream outside or into the kitchen before I throw it in the trash!"

"Aw, Mom," complained Raymond. But, after he'd indulged in a bit more groaning and whining, the boys shuffled off to the backyard.

Chapter Four

The Laundry Room

Left alone again, Annie had some important things to think about. She needed to find a place to spend the night, not to mention that her huge lunch had quite worn off, and she was famished again. First food, then shelter, she reasoned.

Now, in Annie's experience, "mother" meant "food", so she decided to follow the sound of Raymond's mother's voice. Annie stopped short. "Mother," she thought. "Mama!" How she missed her mouse family. How she longed to be back in her cozy, little mouse home in Mr. Dailey's pet shop with Mama and Papa Mouse and Barry, Danny, Carrie and baby Ethel.

Annie paused for a moment, tears welling in her blue eyes, but she pulled herself together. "No, this is no time for daydreaming. I'm an independent mouse," she told herself. "My family doesn't want me and I don't need them, either! I must press on." Annie began crossing the large room, but after a few steps she stopped short. What if that horrifying cat had somehow gotten back into the house? Realizing it was better to stay out of sight as much as possible, she skirted around the edge of the living room, and cautiously entered another room which held a big table and several chairs. She felt fairly safe staying close to the wall, so Annie continued through this next room to pursue the sound of that "motherly" voice, and its promise of possible food.

As she crept along, Annie heard a high-pitched ringing sound coming from around the corner, followed by Raymond's mother's voice. "Hello? Oh, hi, Marge. Yes . . . uh huh. I can . . . sure. Don't you worry about a thing." Annie was looking out across a large, shiny, slippery-looking floor. And there stood Raymond's mother, cradling to her ear, and talking to, a small, black rectangle.

"That must be Marge," Annie thought. While Raymond's mother was engrossed in telling Marge that Zach could sleep over that night, the little mouse decided that speed was wiser than caution at the moment, wanting to get through that room as quickly as possible. After all, what posed more of a risk — a possible cat, or a definite human? Annie stepped out onto the shiny floor and set off running as fast as she could go.

All of a sudden, her mouse paws slipped out from under her, and she found herself sliding and spinning crazily across the slick kitchen floor, right under Mrs. Ratchet's nose.

"Yikes!" Raymond's mother cried, glaring at the swirling mouse. "I'll have to call you back, Marge." "Marge" was tossed rudely down into a leather bag on the counter, and Mrs. Ratchet sped for the back kitchen door. "Raymond Ratchet, get in here this instant!" Before the boy could question her demand with more than a couple of words, his mother shot back with, "Because I said so. That mouse of yours is running amok through my kitchen!"

With a whoop and a holler, the boys came careening through the back door, eager to capture their forgotten prey. By this time, Annie had come to a halt under the kitchen table, as she tried unsuccessfully to maintain a forward momentum. She just couldn't seem to get a grip on that slippery vinyl floor, and every time she'd manage to run a few paces, her paws would again shoot out from under her.

Raymond lunged under the table as soon as he caught sight of Annie. In his haste, he let go of his almost-finished ice cream cone, and it hit the floor right under her whiskers. Annie shot forward, sinking ankle deep into the spreading strawberry puddle. Her feet now coated with the sticky ice cream, she was able to grip the floor. As Raymond grabbed for her, she darted out of his reach and up one of the kitchen table legs. Annie scrambled across the tablecloth, clinking around silverware and skimming over china plates, leaving tiny ice cream footprints in her wake. Just as Raymond's mother was about to swat Annie with a broom, the little mouse hopped down onto a chair, then to the floor, and fled across the far side of the room on her still sticky paws. Mrs. Ratchet was not at all pleased that her attempt to stop the little mouse had resulted only in her smashing a dinner plate and scattering several utensils across the table.

Seeing the door to another room just ahead, Annie rocketed through it and into a murky half-darkness. Hearing the boys close behind her, she leaped into the nearest pile of dirty clothes. Raymond flicked on the overhead light in the laundry room, and he and Zach began flinging dirty jeans and towels over their shoulders.

"There it is, under those underpants!" shrieked Raymond's mother, standing on a step-stool near the doorway.

Annie dug deeper into the laundry pile, as the boys tossed clothes in every direction. To her horror, the little mouse felt herself being lifted into the air, inside a tangled t-shirt. She didn't move a muscle as the shirt was flung aloft, along with other laundry items. She didn't make a sound as she and the t-shirt landed on top of another pile of clothes a few feet away. Thinking fast, Annie quickly extricated herself from the smelly shirt and pawed her way into this pile. With a surge of hope, Annie soon felt the cool, dull linoleum of the laundry room floor under her paws. With shirts and shorts dragging at her fur, she pressed forward toward the wall. Just a few seconds more, and she felt the wall with her tensed whiskers. She made a sharp left turn and began scuttling along the baseboard, under cover of low-hanging jackets and backpacks.

"If you let that vermin run loose in this house, you've had it, Mister," Raymond's distraught mother admonished.

"I don't see him anywhere," whined Raymond.

"Look! The door to the garage is open," said Zach. "Maybe he ran out there."

Both boys tumbled into the garage, where they spent quite a while making a huge racket and a serious mess, before abandoning their search. Raymond's mother went back to the kitchen, closing the laundry room door nervously behind her.

Annie, her heartbeat just beginning to return to normal, had found refuge under a large shelf-unit filled with canned goods and other foodstuffs. Happily for the little mouse, Raymond's mother used the laundry room as a pantry, as well. Sniffing cautiously around on the floor in the semidarkness, she came upon the makings of a meager meal. One crushed corn chip would have to suffice for the time being, since she was in no frame of mind to stray from her hiding place until she was sure that Raymond had abandoned his search. After her light dinner, Annie constructed a makeshift bed for herself out of several dust bunnies and an old sock, trying not to think about how she'd much rather be cuddling up with her parents and her warm, furry brothers and sisters all around her. "Too bad they didn't care to keep me," she mused, as she drifted off to sleep.

Chapter Five

The Spiders

When she awoke, Annie peeked out from under the shelf. There was bright sunlight streaming through the opening under the closed laundry room door. She'd slept all night. Her stomach rumbled. "I'm hungry," the little mouse thought. Annie could hear muffled footsteps and conversation coming from behind the door to the kitchen, but she didn't detect the sharp sound of Raymond's voice.

Annie hated to leave her safe little nest, but, since the growling noises from her tummy were becoming insistent, she decided to risk leaving her hiding place to hunt for food. She didn't have to look far. Almost every shelf in the laundry room was lined with cans, jars, boxes and bags of food. The hungry mouse quickly found out the hard way that she could not open a can with her teeth, nor could she make a dent in any of the hard plastic containers or glass jars, but the boxes and bags were a cinch! Her sharp little front teeth scissored right through all sorts of food packages, and she was soon trying a taste here and a nibble there of various new and exciting treats. Before she finally made herself stop, Annie had eaten one bite from each of a dozen Oreo cookies, two peanuts without shells, and half of the powdered cheese packet from a box of macaroni and cheese. The laundry room would definitely be her new home away from home.

As Annie was just finishing her big breakfast, she froze inside the macaroni box, hearing evidence of humans close by. She listened tensely as one Ratchet after another came tramping through the laundry room and out into the garage, all on their way to work or summer camp. Annie listened carefully to hear the garage doors rumble down and both cars disappear down the driveway. The little mouse hopped down from the bottom shelf and headed for the opening under the door to the kitchen. It was a tight squeeze after her sumptuous breakfast, but Annie soon found herself standing once again on the slippery kitchen floor. She discovered that she could move across it quite efficiently, even though her paws were no longer coated with ice cream, as long as she didn't hurry.

After carefully crossing the kitchen, she scampered through the carpeted dining room and living room, back to the front hall where she'd landed the afternoon before. This time, she noticed a wide-open doorway in the hall. She crept to its edge, and peered into a room much smaller than the others she'd seen. Annie found herself looking straight up at a towering white chair. Because of its slick surface, she wasn't able to climb it, but she scampered up the wall next to it and hopped down onto the chair's top shelf. Looking down on the seat of the chair, she saw that it had a huge oval hole in it, through which she could see a pool of bright, blue water. "Oh, how pretty," thought Annie.

Being interested in exploring the rest of the room at the moment, Annie ran back down the wall. She crossed the small room to its only other piece of furniture. This appeared, from her point of view, to consist only of two wooden doors, one of which had been left ajar. Climbing up onto the low shelf beyond the doors, Annie looked around. She discovered some very thin paper, which had been rolled up onto a gray cardboard tube. Annie thought some of this soft paper would make a lovely addition to her new bed in the laundry room. She also came upon a rectangular cardboard box, which she hoped would contain some food, but all it had inside was layers of more thin white paper.

The little mouse made her way toward the back of the cabinet, sniffing here and there. She stopped dead in her tracks as she heard a strange whispering sound. Annie felt sure that someone was watching her. Slowly, slowly, she turned her head, and found she was staring straight up into the face of a beautiful, round spider. In fact, she was looking at two spiders. The larger of the two was the color of a summer peach — warm yellow with splotches of deep red. The slightly smaller spider was all one color — a cool, misty green. Annie saw that the spiders were hanging from a web attached to some twisting silver pipes, and they seemed to be whispering about her!

"Yessss," hissed one, in a tiny, airy voice.

"Yes, this is the one.

Our job will soon be done."

Annie turned to run, but before she could flee in terror, the other spider murmured in a gossamer-thin voice,

"Please feel no alarm.

We mean you no harm."

"Who . . . who are you?" Annie stammered, turning hesitantly back toward the web and its occupants.

"We're keepers of the secret key,

Which is meant for none but thee," came the whispered answer.

"What key? And what makes you think I'm 'the one'?" Annie asked, feeling very confused.

"The eyes of blue

Gave us the clue," replied the larger spider.

"But what do you mean about a key?" Annie persisted.

"Our conversation now is done.

Come back tomorrow with the sun," was the only answer she was given.

"Wait . . . how . . . why?" Annie was now very agitated, but, without another word, both spiders scuttled up their web and disappeared into a hole behind the cabinet.

"Fine!" Annie said to the empty web. "Why should you help me any more than anyone else has?" But as she made her way back to the laundry room, the little mouse couldn't help feeling excited about this mysterious secret key. What adventures might lie ahead tomorrow?

Chapter Six

The Tasks

After a quick breakfast of several bites from three different donuts, Annie waited eagerly, under cover of the pantry shelves, for the last sounds of the Ratchets leaving the house. She could hardly wait to return to the mysterious creatures in the small room in the front hall.

As she scooted up onto the shelf beyond the open wooden doors in the little room, Annie saw that the spiders had spun their web up toward the front of the cabinet. They were waiting for her there.

"I've very much been looking forward to meeting you again," said Annie. "I believe you were going to tell me something about a secret key."

"You must master tasks of three,

Before you will obtain the key," whispered the green spider.

Annie was brimming with questions. "What sort of tasks? Where will I go? When will I go? And what kind of key is it?"

Before Annie could take a breath and begin with another round of questions, the red and yellow spider held up one of her arms for silence.

"Each step will be revealed in time.

We'll give you every task in rhyme," she murmured.

"That will be lovely, thank you," said Annie. "But please, I must know what the key is for! Does it unlock a door? A treasure chest?"

"The key will unlock something higher.

It is your heart's fondest desire," whispered the green spider.

"Oh, I see," replied Annie. To herself, she added "I have only one 'fondest desire', and that's for my family to love me and for us to be together again. I can't imagine that's possible." Just in case it was, however, she was anxious to get started on her quest. She hoped that sitting quietly would signal to the spiders that she was ready to be given her first assignment. She waited only moments.

"When you hear the human's voice,
You will have to make a choice.
Come out into the human's view,
Or the key will never come to you.
Return tomorrow, and then ask
Directions for your second task."

Having said this, the spiders turned without another word and silently crawled along the silk threads of their web, disappearing into the shadows.

Annie hopped down from the cabinet and slowly retraced her steps to her new little home in the laundry room. "Gosh," she said in disappointment. "What kind of a task is that? I thought they were going to give me a real job to do . . . maybe find a treasure or fight a monster. Why in the world would they want me to come out from hiding and allow Raymond and his family to see me? They'd just put me back in that tank!"

As Annie reached her sock-bed under the laundry room shelf, she flopped down on top of it. She closed her bright, blue eyes, and lay there thinking and wondering. "No use just stewing and fretting," the little mouse chided herself. "That doesn't do anything but get me more upset and confused."

In order to calm herself down and start planning constructively, Annie thought about all the things she was grateful for, a habit that Mrs. Mouse had taught all her children. Annie was very grateful for her mouse family, and for the life she'd had with them before they'd allowed her to be taken away. She was grateful that she had all this lovely food to eat, any time she was hungry. And, as she turned over on her homemade bed, Annie realized that she was grateful for this old sock, too. As Annie buried her nose in the soft, white folds of her sock-bed, a clever plan began to hatch in her little mouse head.

Chapter Seven

The Disguise

Annie lay on her bed thinking and planning for quite a while. "I'm sure the spiders didn't mean for me to be captured, since they told me to come back tomorrow," she assured herself. "They said I'd have to come out into view," she reasoned, "but they never said that the Ratchets would have to know it was me they were seeing. If I could put my bed over me as a disguise, all they'd see would be an old sock."

Annie pulled her sock-bed out from under the shelf and crawled beneath it. The sock began inching around the floor in the laundry room, as Annie practiced moving ever so slowly. If she kept the toe raised just slightly, she was able to see where she was going.

When she felt that she had her plan all in order and had practiced sufficiently at moving like a sock, Annie crept back under her shelf to wait for the sounds of humans. Before long, a car pulled into the garage. Mrs. Ratchet, followed by Raymond, came into the laundry room, heading for the kitchen. Raymond tossed his backpack carelessly at a hook on the wall as he passed through. The backpack hit the floor, and Raymond's sweatshirt joined it, preventing the door to the kitchen from closing when he gave it a heedless backward kick. Annie could faintly hear Raymond's feet pounding up the stairs to his room, as Mrs. Ratchet set about preparing dinner in the kitchen.

Annie cautiously peeked out from her hiding place, and crept toward the kitchen door, under cover of the sock. Now would be a great time for her to perform her task, with Raymond occupied upstairs. Annie skirted around the abandoned sweatshirt and sneaked up to the open door. It would have been nearly impossible to implement her plan if she'd had to get her sock through the narrow space under the closed door without being seen. "Thank goodness for Raymond's sloppy habits," she thought.

Annie raised the toe of her disguise just a teensy bit, in order to make sure that she was seeing the backs of Mrs. Ratchet's high-heeled shoes. Sure enough, Raymond's mother was facing the stove and humming over a sizzling frying pan. The little mouse tiptoed a few inches into the room and halted. Peering out again to be sure that her movements weren't being observed, Annie advanced further into the kitchen. As she peeked out a third time, Annie saw the high-heels turn and face her. She held her breath and didn't move a mouse muscle, as Mrs. Ratchet walked straight toward her.

"That boy," Raymond's mother was saying. "Will he ever learn to pick up after himself? Look at this sock in the middle of the kitchen floor."

Annie thought her heart would stop, as she made desperate plans to run for her life. But just as Mrs. Ratchet's fingers were about to brush the tips of Annie's whiskers, the woman straightened up. "No, I guess he won't ever learn if I keep picking up for him," she said, turning to leave the room. While Raymond's mother was busy yelling up the stairs for her son to come down and put away his belongings, Annie bolted back to the laundry room as fast as she and her sock-bed could go. She scooted under the shelf, whipping her bed in behind her, and waited, trembling and listening.

After a few minutes, she heard Raymond's grating voice. "What sock? I don't see any sock."

"And pick up your backpack while you're at it," came Mrs. Ratchet's annoyed half shout from upstairs.

"Okay, okay!" Raymond yelled back. And

then "Stupid backpack! Why don't you stay on the hook when I put you there?"

There was a bit of stamping and shuffling as Raymond returned his errant backpack to its proper place, and Annie watched with whiskers tensed as Raymond approached the pantry shelf under which she hid. He grabbed at a plastic jar, twisted off the lid and stuck two of his fingers inside, lifting a glob of light brown paste into his mouth.

"Raymond, stay out of the peanut butter!" came Mrs. Ratchet's voice from the other room. Raymond quickly tossed the jar and its unattached lid back onto the shelf, and the laundry room door was slammed pointedly, leaving Annie alone in her bedroom once again.

The little mouse lay on her disheveled bed for quite a while, relishing her success with the sock, yet wondering why she'd been given such an odd task. She'd have to ask the spiders tomorrow, she decided. As she drifted off to sleep, her last thought was to wonder if this secret key could really unlock her fondest desire.

Chapter Eight

The Peanut Butter

Annie awoke the next morning to the sound of heavy rain pounding on the laundry room roof. It somewhat muffled the sounds of the Ratchets going about their usual morning activities in the kitchen. After a good bit of anxious waiting for the family to leave for the day, Annie realized that the morning routine was dragging on much longer than it usually did. Little did Annie realize that today was Saturday, and, it being such a rainy Saturday, the Ratchets weren't going anywhere.

Annie waited for hours for the garage door to open and the cars to pull down the driveway, before she finally faced the fact that she would not be making a trip to the spiders' room in the hall that day. Since the humans' voices had been coming and going through the kitchen door all morning, she couldn't risk trying to go across that slick kitchen floor.

Since Annie had had quite enough of "coming out of hiding" the day before, she decided to make the best of the situation, and spend some time exploring right there in the laundry room. She climbed up and poked around in Raymond's half-open backpack, but all she found in there was a huge wad of crumpled papers and a ham and cheese sandwich that was so old even she wasn't interested.

She did find something that pleased her, though, in an old paper bag behind the shelf. It was a tangle of soft, white string, which she thought would make a comfy stuffing for her sock-bed. The dust bunnies had been making her sneeze, and she'd forgotten to bring some of the soft paper from the cabinet in the spiders' room, so she was happy to find another filler for her bed.

In her previous investigations of the many wonderful foods that stocked the laundry room shelves, Annie had come to automatically avoid anything in a can or a jar. When she came to Raymond's abandoned peanut butter jar, the hungry mouse couldn't believe her luck at finding it resting on its side with its lid lying beside it. After sniffing its heavenly aroma, Annie dove headfirst into her delectable discovery. She tunneled into the creamy center of the jar and wiggled around in glee. She ate and ate, and slithered around, and ate some more.

Before she knew it, Annie had consumed a hefty portion of that little jar of peanut butter. When she finally dragged herself back to its rim, she found that she could barely move. As she hung lethargically over the edge of the jar, Annie was horrified to see the door to the laundry room opening. Since she was in no condition to move quickly; all she could do was stay still and not move even a whisker. She'd just have to pray that Mrs. Ratchet, who was coming into the laundry room with a large basket of clothes, would not notice her.

"Oh please, oh please, oh please," Annie said silently. "Please don't look over this way." She need not have worried, for Mrs. Ratchet was completely absorbed in what she was doing. Thanks to Raymond's nasty habit of tossing dirty laundry onto the floor, anyone coming into the room, especially when carrying a large overflowing basket, had to watch very carefully where they were walking.

Annie observed in fascination, despite her trepidation, as Mrs. Ratchet put the laundry basket on a huge, white, square piece of furniture and began a strange ritual. Next to that was another huge, white square, with a large hole in its top. Into this hole Raymond's mother was stuffing most of the clothing. Onto them she poured a cup of thick, blue liquid. Annie observed as Mrs. Ratchet closed a hinged lid down on top of the clothes and pressed some buttons on the back of the square. A terrible rumbling and splashing noise came from the box. Annie had never witnessed anything like this before, and found the sound of it quite unnerving. She watched nervously as Mrs. Ratchet turned to leave the room. Stepping carefully over and around Raymond's cast-off clothing, the busy woman never noticed the immobilized mouse.

Left alone again, Annie turned her attentions to her predicament. "You've got to get up!" Annie said to herself, although she was feeling extremely sluggish. "It's not safe to stay here!" With tremendous effort, Annie wobbled and dragged herself back down to her sock-bed, leaving smears and prints of peanut butter behind her. Finally, she eased herself into the folds of her bed, feeling the need to nurse her too-full tummy. As the little mouse turned over with a groan, Mrs. Ratchet came purposefully back into the laundry room. This time, her eyes went straight to the opened peanut butter jar.

"Will you look at that," she said, picking up the jar. "RayMOND!!"

Noticing the tiny peanut butter paw prints on the shelf, Raymond's mother let out another shriek. "I knew that darned mouse was still around!" she cried. "That's it. I'm calling Mr. Bernard!"

Annie could only wonder who this Mr. Bernard might be, as she carefully groomed her fur, licking off the last, no-longer-tantalizing traces of peanut butter.

Chapter Nine

The Pool

Late the following morning, Annie awoke with a still-very-full tummy. She decided to skip breakfast, and go right to the spiders' room, hoping they'd be understanding about her missed appointment the day before. Happily, it was Sunday, and the sun was shining bright. Annie didn't know it, but, as she'd slept soundly all morning in her peanut-butter-induced stupor, the Ratchets had all gone off to church, which would be followed by a picnic.

Hearing no trace of human voices, Annie peeked out from under her shelf. What a relief to see that the door to the kitchen had been left wide open. It would have been quite uncomfortable to squeeze beneath the door in her current state. She walked through the kitchen, wobbled through the dining room and practically rolled down the hall, impatient to hear of her next task. However, when she got just inside the door to the small room in the hall, Annie met with a sight that made her heart sink. Although they'd always been left ajar before, the cabinet doors were shut tight. Try as she might, the tiny mouse couldn't make those huge doors budge. How would she ever get inside to talk to the spiders? They'd think that she didn't care about completing her tasks. She'd never get the secret key, or even find out for sure what it was! What was she to do?

Just as Annie was about to turn away in despair, she heard that now-familiar whispering sound. Where was it coming from? Annie looked all around her, and, as she looked straight up, she saw both spiders looking down at her from the top of the cabinet. "Oh, good morning," Annie said quickly. "I'm so sorry about yesterday. I couldn't get out of the laundry room, because the Ratchets were around all day, and. . . ."

The larger spider interrupted in her airy voice, which magically carried all the way down to the floor, despite its lack of volume.

"Your task for yesterday, you set yourself.
You learned a valued lesson on the shelf."

"I can't argue with that," said Annie, as her stomach gurgled, reminding her of how unpleasant she'd felt after eating so much peanut butter the day before.

"Speaking of tasks, if you don't mind," the

mouse continued, "I was wondering if you could tell me the reason for my first task. It seemed such a strange thing to ask, and I was just, well, wondering. . . ," she petered out.

"Once you have obtained the key

In mortal danger you may be.

These tasks will help you to prepare

To skirt the danger, and beware," was the larger spider's response.

Annie didn't spend any time worrying about what that "mortal danger" might be, so eager was she to learn of her next task. "So, what have you got for me to do today?" she asked.

"Your task for today

Is not far away," said the smaller spider.

"Find a pool the color of your eyes.

You must cross it and you must stay dry," said her companion.

"I know!" chirped Annie. "That pretty bathing pool under the hole in the white chair!" Forgetting about her full tummy, she dashed up the wall and onto the top shelf of the toilet. There, below, was the shining blue pool. But how would she ever be able to get to it? The back of the chair went straight down and was even more slippery than the kitchen floor.

Annie noticed a small, silver ledge on the top left corner of the chair. Maybe she could step down onto that and jump from there to the seat. As she let her weight down onto the silver platform, it began to tip. Before she could back up and restore the platform to its upright position, a terrible whooshing and roaring sound came from the pool below. As Annie looked down in terror, she saw the blue water rushing up toward the seat, and receding in a raging whirlpool. Leaping back onto the top of the chair on quivering legs, Annie realized that the treacherous descent to the pool was not her only problem.

Chapter Ten

The Crossing

"It looks like that mortal danger the spiders were talking about might be right here already!" Annie thought to herself. "I don't see how I could conceivably get down there and cross that wild water," she worried silently.

Aloud, she asked in a shaky voice, "If the blue water might surge up like that at any moment, how could I possibly swim across it?"

Looking over at the spiders as they watched her from their perch on top of the sink, she saw that one of them was about to speak.

"We choose not our words on a whim.
When did we utter the word 'swim'?"

"Oh, I guess I could make a boat!" Annie responded. "But how could I get it down there, and what if the water rose up again and knocked me out of it?"

"What is the need to make a boat?
When did we utter the word 'float'?"

"Let's see," said Annie. "What were those

exact words?" She closed her blue eyes and thought very hard, straining to remember. As she listened inside herself quietly, the words came back one by one.

"Find a pool the color of your eyes.

You must cross it and you must stay dry."

"Cross it. Cross it," Annie said to herself. "I get it!" she squealed. "I don't have to swim in the water, or even float on it to cross the pool. I just have to find a way to get across this hole in the seat, and I'll be crossing above the water!" She looked over and saw the spiders applauding with all sixteen of their tiny hands.

Annie looked down at the hole in the chair seat, attempting to gauge its width.

"I'm not sure I could jump that far," Annie called over to the spiders. "I can jump down, but I don't know if I can jump across things."

"Use what you have and what you know,

And you will find a way to go," they answered.

"Well," said Annie, "all I have in the world is my little sock-bed under the laundry room shelf, and a wad of string. Hmm, string. . . ." Her whiskers quivered as an idea formed.

"I could tie the string to the silver platform, and. . . ." Without finishing her thought, Annie went tripping down the wall, out into the hall, and off to her bedroom.

She was back in a flash, trailing her new collection of string behind her. She hauled it up onto the top of the toilet, and set to work tying the string to the silver platform, very carefully, so as not to make it tip. When she'd secured a sturdy knot, Annie lowered herself down the string an inch or two to see if it could bear her weight. "This will do just fine," she thought, as she shimmied back up to the top of the chair. Now Annie knew that she could get down to the seat, but she still had no idea of how to get across the hole and over the water.

"Use what I know," she mused aloud. "I know that peanut butter is very tasty, unless you eat so much that it hurts." She looked across to see the spiders tapping their feet and shaking their heads. "Okay, think, Annie, think," she said to herself, and her little whiskers vibrated in earnest. It occurred to Annie that, since this white chair was something used by the humans, she'd have to use her knowledge about some other human contraption. "The string is the newest thing that I have, so maybe I need to use the newest thing that I know," she reasoned. "What did I see in the laundry room yesterday?" she asked herself, closing her blue eyes so she could concentrate. "I saw Raymond's mother hide the clothes in the big, white noise-making machine. It had a hole in it just like this chair, and Mrs. Ratchet pulled a white lid down onto it. I wonder. . . ."

When Annie opened her eyes she jumped with delight. There, right under her whiskers, she saw that this chair also had a lid for the hole in its seat, and she just hadn't noticed it before. Not only that — the lid for the seat was so tall that it reached right up to the top of the toilet, and she could go right over and put her paws on it. "I'll bet if I gave this lid a shove, it would close right down over the hole," she thought. And that is exactly what happened, as the lid came down with a resounding crash that echoed through the house. "Thank goodness none of the Ratchets are home," Annie called over to the spiders, who waved in agreement.

When she saw that the hole was covered, the excited little mouse slid down her string in one shot. As she nearly reached the end of the string, she heard the frightening sound of the rushing blue water again, but she plopped down safely onto the closed lid and walked across it, far above the whirlpool. Annie turned to see the spiders nodding their congratulations.

"You've worked and thought hard
and completed your task.

No more for today

will your spider friends ask," they whispered, and they scuttled down into the sink, and out of sight.

"Phew!" thought Annie. "I'm ready to go have a snack." So that is what she did. As she lay in her little bed later that night, Annie's thoughts churned with questions about the secret key, the unknown mortal danger that could follow, and her third and final task for tomorrow.

Chapter Eleven

The Sink

The next morning, Annie found herself wondering worriedly about what her third task would entail. Nevertheless, as she finished her breakfast of pretzels and crackers (with no peanut butter) she couldn't help entering into the spirit of anticipation, as she reminded herself that completion of today's task would bring her knowledge of the secret key.

As Annie entered the small room in the hall, she saw that today the doors to the cabinet were once again shut tight. She looked hopefully up toward the top ledge of the cabinet, but no spiders were in evidence.

"Hello!" Annie called. "Please! I can't get inside the doors!"

As she had the other day, Annie tried with all her might to pry the doors open with her little paws, but, as before, they wouldn't budge. She tried calling again, but no spidery forms appeared above.

"I have to figure out how to get to the spiders," the little mouse told herself. "I can't possibly allow another day of delay. I want that secret key!"

With that, Annie set about examining the huge doors looming above her, searching for some way to get them open. She knew she could find a way. Hadn't she figured out how to get across the blue pool yesterday?

The doors had no handles, nothing she could pull on, even if she could reach up that high. She did notice indentations at the very top of each door, where human fingers could get a grip and pull them open, but nothing she could get her paws around, even if she was up on top of the cabinet.

"That's it!" Annie cried. "I saw the spiders on top of the cabinet the other day. If they could get to the top of the cabinet from their hiding place, maybe I can get to them from there!" The little mouse scampered up the front of the wooden doors, easily digging her needle-sharp claws into the painted wooden surface. Before she knew it, she was peering down into the bowl of the sink.

As she looked around, Annie saw two small holes near the top of the sink. "I could never fit through those," she realized immediately. At the base of the bowl, she saw a circular opening, edged in shiny silver metal. Annie quickly slid down the side of the bowl and began sniffing at the hole. On closer inspection, she saw that it was topped with a metal disc, which was elevated only enough to leave a small opening. The spiders could possibly fit through that space, she surmised, but there was no way a mouse could squeeze through.

"All right," Annie said, with determination. "I'll just move this round thing out of the way." She pushed on the sink stopper with all of her might. She bit it with her teeth and clawed it with her paws, to no avail. Nearly exhausted, Annie lay down on the floor of the sink to catch her breath. "I will do this. I will do this. I WILL DO THIS!" she said with great conviction, her voice echoing into the hole that lay just a whisker's breadth from her nose.

As her words died away, Annie heard a strange scrambling sound. To her amazement, the spiders began to push their way into the sink from the two small holes near the top of the bowl, and soon they were standing right before her.

"Oh, I'm so happy to see you!" Annie squealed. "I've been trying to get to you, and the doors were closed, and I couldn't get through the hole, and. . . ."

The smaller spider held up one hand.

"We heard your call and felt your will.

Your heart and strength will aid you still," she whispered.

"Why, yes, I believe they will," Annie said thoughtfully. "So," she added quickly, "Are you ready to give me my final task?"

Chapter Twelve

The Table

Both spiders stepped forward, nodding in the affirmative.

"Go down below and choose from three.

A good friend is what you must be," were their cryptic words to her.

"Why do I have to be somebody's friend?" Annie wanted to know. "I don't need any friends. I can get along just fine by myself," she insisted. She knew she was being hardhearted, but that was better than being hurt again, wasn't it? Mr. Daily had sold her, her family had let her go, and Raymond Ratchet had left her to starve. "Why should I expect some 'friend' to treat me any better?" the sad little mouse asked herself.

When the spiders made no response to her spoken question, she thanked them briefly anyway, and started off, puzzling over their instructions. "Go down below," repeated Annie, as she stepped out into the hallway. "I thought I was already downstairs." As she proceeded through the hallway, however, farther than she'd ever gone before, Annie found herself facing a different set of steps, which led to the basement. "Oh, I know how to do this," she thought, and began a careful backward climb, step by step, just as she'd done on her first day of freedom.

On reaching the bottom, Annie looked around in the near darkness, and saw three doors — one on each side, and one straight ahead. Each one had been left ajar. "Ah, choose from three," she thought. "How shall I choose?" she wondered. The doors all looked exactly the same. This time, the spiders were not watching from across the way, ready to steer her in the right direction. "Well, I always want to do what's right, so I suppose I should take the door on the right," she reasoned with her mouse logic. So, forging bravely ahead, Annie crept through the door on the right and entered a room even larger than the living room upstairs.

In the shadowy stillness, Annie saw a huge shape looming above her in the dim light from the small basement windows. This shape seemed to be a large table. Always willing to pursue the possibility of finding food, she decided to investigate, and scurried up one of its legs. On reaching the top, Annie saw that this table was not set with dishes and utensils like the one in the kitchen, but instead was scattered with shiny balls. As she nudged one, it rolled into another ball with a sharp clacking sound. She gave a heftier shove to another ball, which sailed across the table and disappeared into a hole at the table's edge. This was fun! Temporarily forgetting about her given task, Annie was soon scurrying all over the table, knocking balls here and there, and watching them disappear down the holes.

Before she knew it, all the balls were gone. "Well," she said to herself, "I'll have to climb down into one of those holes and bring some balls back up. This is much too much fun to stop now." Annie stuck her whiskers into the nearest hole, but, before she could begin to climb in, she was startled by a shrill little voice.

"Hey! What do you think you're doing? You almost crushed me with those balls!"

Annie jerked backward on the table, and was amazed to see a small head pop up out of the hole which she'd been about to enter.

"This is my playground! What are you doing here?" The head was soon followed by a whole hamster, who approached Annie menacingly.

"I . . . I'm so sorry," said Annie, backing away. "I didn't know anybody lived here in this table."

"I don't live here, you ninny! I live over there between the walls," said the angry hamster, jerking his head toward the back wall of the big room. "I just come up here to play when no humans are around. And I'll thank you not to go rolling those balls around on the roof and shoving them into the hallways when I'm trying to play!"

"Oh, of course," said Annie, and she hurried back toward the edge of the table. But the little mouse halted halfway across. Her curiosity was stronger than her fear. "If you please," she squeaked out as she turned back, "before I go, could you tell me how you came to be living down here?"

"If it'll make you scram, I'll tell you," said the hamster. "That Raymond boy bought me so long ago I can't remember when, and he put me in an old fish tank in his room way upstairs. He quit feeding me and playing with me, so I had to get myself out of the tank and go find my own food. One day, Raymond tossed one of his shirts over the edge of the tank, and I just climbed up it and got out."

"Lucky you," Annie said, half to herself, remembering her frightening cat encounter.

"What?"

"Oh, nothing. I'm sorry. Please go on."

"Well, anyway, as I was saying," he continued,

"after they stopped looking for me and forgot about me, I found my way down here.

"I've been living here all by myself ever since. Every once in a while, they come down here to play with the balls, and I have to lay low, but usually I have the place to myself, and that's the way I like it. I don't like visitors, and I don't like anybody, see?"

"Oh . . . oh dear," said Annie, reaching her paw out instinctively toward the hamster.

"Cut the mushy act," he grumbled. "I don't want your sympathy, and I don't want your company, so just steer clear. Got it?"

"Certainly," said Annie, "if you're sure. . . ."

"GET LOST!"

And with that, Annie bolted over the side of the table and streaked across the room toward the same door she'd entered earlier.

Chapter Thirteen

The Gift

"**O**h my," thought Annie, as she rested on the third step. "That poor hamster! I'm all for independence, but he's carrying it a bit too far. He really needs a friend." Her heart sank. Could the spiders possibly have meant for her to make friends with him? This made the first two tasks seem simple!

"He's probably just cranky because he hasn't had anyone to love him in a long time," Annie decided. "I know how that feels," she sighed. "I'll just go right back in there and talk to him in a friendly way, and maybe even give him a hug." She was willing to try anything to get that secret key!

Full of determination, the little mouse ran back to the table and scooted up one of its legs. She marched over to the hole where she'd last seen the hamster, and knocked on the wood next to it. When her knocking met no response, she called down the hole.

"Mr. Hamster . . . hello . . . are you there?"

Like a jack-in-the-box, the hamster came shooting out of the hole again, nearly knocking Annie off her feet.

"My name is not Mr. Hamster, it's Benjie. And I thought I told you to steer clear, didn't I?"

"Well, yes," said Annie, flustered. "It's just that I thought. . . ."

"You thought. You thought. Who told you to think about me? Now vamoose, before I bowl you over with one of these balls."

With that, Benjie started shoving the balls he'd already brought back up onto the table, rolling them fast toward Annie with all his might.

As one of the balls missed Annie's hindquarters by a whisker's width, she decided she'd better be on her way. Turning to get one last look at her intended friend, Annie saw a shiny, red ball coming straight for her at breakneck speed. She dodged out of its way, and leaped over the side of the table one more time, heading for the stairs. This time she made it to the top before she stopped to catch her breath. "I'll just have to ask the spiders to choose another friend for me," she resolved, heading for the cabinet in the small room.

Annie should have guessed that her request would be met merely with shaking heads and poetry.

"A friendship made in the proper way

Is not likely won in just one day," was all that the spiders said before they disappeared into the hole behind the silver pipes.

Annie felt heavy disappointment as she realized that she would not be winning the secret key that day. Making a friend was turning into the most difficult task of all.

When Annie got back to her little home under the laundry room shelf, she settled down to a hearty dinner and a good long think. There must be a way to get through to that unhappy hamster. It had to be done if she was ever going to get the secret key.

"I'll bet I could tempt Benjie with something good to eat. He looked so skinny and scruffy. He must be awfully hungry," Annie thought, as she licked the last crumbs from a bag of dried fruit. The only things left in the bag were all the prune pieces, since Annie didn't at all enjoy the taste of prunes.

"Maybe I could bring Benjie all these prunes. Then they wouldn't be wasted," she mused. "Oh, but that's no way to make a friend," Annie realized. "I should bring him what I like best!" And with that, Annie set about roaming up and down all the pantry shelves, sniffing here and scrutinizing there, trying to decide what would be the most wonderful gift for her prospective friend.

On the bottom shelf, at the back of a thin, white cardboard box with red and blue words on it, she saw it — two lovely, pink cupcakes, completely wrapped in clear plastic. They each had a squiggle of white icing across their pink frosted tops, and they sat side by side on a shiny, white rectangle of cardboard. Annie didn't think she'd ever seen anything more beautiful. This is what she must offer to the lonely hamster. Surely, Benjie's spirits would lift at the sight of this marvelous treat! Pulling at the plastic wrapping as delicately as she could with her sharp, little teeth, Annie dragged her precious find down under the shelf and set it next to her bed, ready for delivery the next day.

Chapter Fourteen

The Friend

In the morning, as soon as Annie heard the last human footsteps leave the house and the last car start up and fade away, she set about her task of bringing her offering to Benjie. She didn't even stop by the cabinet in the small room to check in with the spiders. Sliding the wrapped cupcakes across the slippery kitchen floor was a breeze, but, when she reached the dining room carpet, the going got tougher. Annie had to drag the package, inch by inch, over the rough, bumpy surface, stopping to rest every few feet.

When she finally reached the top of the basement steps, she halted in dismay. Was there an easy way to get her special cargo down the long flight of stairs? When she thought of just shoving them over the edge, and letting the cupcakes tumble down on their own, she visualized the dented wreck she'd find at the bottom and decided against it. She'd just have to face the fact that she had a long, hard job ahead of her.

Annie took a few deep breaths, squared her shoulders, and began dragging the cupcakes, step by step, down the long flight of stairs. She'd climb halfway down each step, reach up to catch the cupcake wrapper in her teeth, and then lower it as gently as possible to the next step below. Over and over she followed this same tiring procedure, until she was faint with the effort. Eleven times she climbed, grabbed and lowered, climbed, grabbed and lowered.

When Annie and the cupcakes reached the basement, she was more tired than she'd ever imagined a mouse could be. "I certainly hope this friendship thing is worth all the effort," she complained to herself. With her last bit of strength, Annie pulled her pretty pink burden out into the middle of the floor in the big room and flopped down next to it, exhausted. How long she lay there, too weary to move, she didn't know.

Presently, she was jarred to alertness by a strident voice.

"Watcha' got there?"

Annie rolled over quickly and looked up into the face of Benjie. "It's a present," she said, trying to hide her surprise at seeing him there in the middle of the room.

"What kind of present? Who's it for,

anyway?" he demanded.

"Why, it's a 'let's be friends' present, and it's for you," Annie offered.

At that, Benjie closed his eyes, put his paws up over his face, and started to cry. He cried so hard, he had to lie down on the ground and cry some more.

"If you don't like it, I can find something else," said Annie, distraught over the hamster's reaction. "I'm sorry," she apologized. "I thought you would like it because I liked it so much myself when I found it."

"I . . . I do like it," sobbed Benjie. "It's j-just that nobody has ever given me a present before."

"There, there, now," crooned Annie, as she stroked Benjie's furry head.

"I'm here. You have a friend, now. My name is Annie. And we'll give each other presents all the time, if you like." She hoped this sounded convincing.

Benjie hiccuped a few times and dried his eyes. He almost started to cry all over again, as he gulped out, "B-but I don't have anything to give you. All I have is those noisy balls, and the little bit of food I can find for myself down here in the basement."

"It's okay," soothed Annie. "You can come upstairs with me. You won't believe how much food there is in the laundry room. That's where I found your present. Why don't you open it?"

Just about fully recovered now, Benjie began to investigate the cupcakes in their wrapping. "Let's open it together," he said, not quite sure how to proceed.

"See, you just tear this clear stuff with your teeth," Annie instructed.

When the plastic had been pulled halfway off the first cake, Benjie stepped back.

"You take the first bite," he offered. "That will be my 'let's be friends' present to you!"

"Oh, thank you," said Annie, and took a dainty nibble of the sweet pink icing.

"Come on. Let's dig in," said the eager hamster, and they were both soon whisker-deep in pink cake and white cream filling. Remembering her less-than-pleasant experience with the aftermath of the peanut butter incident, Annie ate only until she felt that she was full. Then she sat back and enjoyed watching Benjie eat to his heart's content. After all, he'd had nothing good to eat in so long. Before she knew it, he'd eaten every crumb. There was nothing left but the cardboard rectangle and the crumpled plastic wrapper.

Chapter Fifteen

The Stairs

Both hamster and mouse, their tummies contentedly filled, lay on their backs, whiskers touching, and stared at the basement ceiling.

"Do you eat this much all the time?" asked Benjie, after a while.

"Oh, I could if I wanted to," Annie replied. "There's plenty of food to be had upstairs. But I've learned that I should eat only so much at a time. It gets hard to move around if you eat too much at once," she advised.

"I know what you mean," said Benjie, giving a little belch. "And, Annie," he added shyly, "I'm really sorry about throwing those balls at you yesterday. I've been alone so long, I just didn't know how to act. But I got to thinking last night that a friend could be something pretty good."

"I suppose so," said Annie. "I've never really had a friend. I've learned not to depend on anyone too much," she confided. "I guess friends must be good, though, or the spiders wouldn't have told me to find one."

"Spiders?" Benjie squeaked.

"Oh, yes! They're really splendid," Annie replied. "Let's go upstairs and you can meet them right now," she said, heading for the door.

"Wait!" Benjie called, following as Annie scampered off to the staircase. "Aren't spiders scary?"

"Not at all," Annie assured him, pushing the hamster toward the bottom step. "Up you go!" she said encouragingly.

"I . . . I can't. I don't know how," the hamster stammered. "I came down the stairs once, a long time ago, but I've never climbed up," he admitted.

"Going up is almost easier than coming down," Annie explained. "Climb up on my back and you're half way up the first step. Then just hook your claws into the carpet and pull yourself up," she said, giving Benjie's bottom a mighty shove.

"Whoa! Oh, I get it!" the hamster squealed, as he shot up onto the first step. "We can do this together. Now give me your paws and I'll pull you up."

"No, no. I've done this before. I can do it myself," Annie said, as she pulled herself up the steep step.

"Annie, I thought you said we were friends. Don't friends help each other? Doesn't it go both ways?" Benjie asked in a wounded voice.

Annie stopped her ascent and looked at Benjie's woebegone face. "What could it hurt to let him help?" she asked herself.

"Okay, Buddy. Help away!" she said, extending her paw.

With a happy smile and a surprising strength, Benjie lifted his mouse friend easily up onto the step next to him.

"Wow!" said an amazed Annie. "You've got some power in those paws! It really is much easier to climb these stairs with help. Maybe this is one of the reasons the spiders told me to find a friend," she added, giving her companion a push up to the next step.

"Say, about those spiders," Benjie puffed, hauling himself onto the third step. "You're sure they're not dangerous?"

"They're a bit mysterious," replied Annie, as she hoisted Benjie up to the fourth step. "But they're really very smart and helpful. They're going to give me a secret key soon, and I'll be happy to show it to you."

"A key to what?" Benjie asked, clawing his way upward.

"Actually, I don't know that," the little mouse

replied quickly, not yet ready to admit to her hope that the key might somehow reunite her with her family. "But I know it's a key to something extraordinary, because I've had to work very hard to get it."

"Golly!" said Benjie, as he was assisted up to the ninth step. "What will we do after we visit the spiders?"

"By then I should have my key, and who knows what will happen from there!" Annie crowed, not noticing the worried look on Benjie's little face.

After reaching the top, hamster and mouse made their way down the hall to the spiders' room. Annie could hardly hide her annoyance when she saw that the cabinet doors were shut tight. She could not abide any further delay. "Maybe they're sitting up on top," she said to her friend.

"Wait here," she added, when it was clear that they were not. Annie scooted up the cabinet doors and stopped on the sink ledge.

"Annie, what are you doing?" Benjie called. "Please don't leave me alone!"

"I'm just going to yell down the hole and see if the spiders can hear me," Annie said over her shoulder. "Hellooooo! I've finished my tasks and I need my key now!" she called into the hole in the sink. The impatient little mouse listened carefully, but heard no scrambling noises, no whispered greetings.

"Come on, Annie. I'm getting scared," Benjie beckoned from below.

"SSShhhhh! I'm trying to listen," she shot back.

"Sorry," Benjie whimpered.

"SSShhhhh!" Annie repeated.

After several more attempts to summon the spiders, Annie climbed back down to the nervously waiting Benjie, reporting that the spiders were nowhere to be found.

"It's all right," said Benjie, a bit relieved. "We can come back tomorrow."

"Yes, we'll come back tomorrow," Annie said, trying not to let on how bothered she felt about having to wait yet another day to get the secret key. "Let's go to my house and I'll show you around."

Chapter Sixteen

The Visitor

As they exited the small room, Annie heard a terrifying sound. Her mouse ears picked up human footsteps, and a key was being turned in the lock on the front door, not ten feet away from where they stood.

"Run!" she yelled.

With Benjie on her heels, she led him around the corner and into the dining room, as they heard the front door opening.

"Go, go, go!" the little mouse squealed, hearing high-heeled footsteps coming down the hall.

Annie stopped short on the threshold of the kitchen. "We can't run on this floor, or we'll slide out of control," she cried. "And if we walk slowly, they'll catch us for sure!"

Thinking fast, Annie darted back through the corner of the dining room and into the living room. With the hamster close behind her, she raced under the couch and headed for the shadowy safety of the wall behind it.

"Stay quiet!" she warned, and they both remained stock still, listening.

A minute later, they heard the sing-song sound of a bell chiming near the front door. Footsteps hurried past them, and Annie heard Mrs. Ratchet's familiar voice.

"Thanks so much for meeting me here, Mr. Bernard."

"I'm happy to help you get rid of those vermin, ma'am," came a stranger's voice in reply.

Two sets of whiskers quivered in fright, as two sets of shoes walked past the couch and into the kitchen.

"Oh, my. We're vermin!" Annie whispered. "I heard Mrs. Ratchet call me that once."

"You mean they want to get rid of us? That's crazy! What have we done to them?" asked Benjie.

"Maybe it's because I ate a lot of their food," confessed Annie. "But it's Raymond's fault for forgetting to feed me," she added in her own defense.

"Or maybe they're mad because I played with the balls on their table," worried Benjie. He was beginning to wonder if he'd been wise to entrust his safety to this mouse that he barely knew. How could she bring him upstairs among all these dangerous humans?

Annie and Benjie huddled under the couch all afternoon, listening to Mr. Bernard clomping through the house, poking here and banging there. Even after he left, the mouse and the hamster were too scared to risk trying to go through the kitchen to the laundry room. During their hours hidden in the living room, they whispered back and forth, the little mouse telling her new friend all about her experiences with her three tasks. The more he heard of Annie's story, the more Benjie realized that they were both part of something important. Perhaps it would be best to stick with her.

Finally, when all the Ratchets had gone up to bed, they crept out of the living room, through the corner of the dining room, and slowly across the slippery kitchen floor.

"Here we are," said Annie, as they got to the laundry room door. "We just have to squeeze . . . Oh no! What's this?"

Mr. Bernard had attached a long strip of hard rubber along the bottom edge of the door. Pushing, pulling and nibbling with all their might, neither Annie nor Benjie were able to make it budge.

"What will we do?" wailed Annie.

"We should go back down to my house for tonight," offered Benjie. "There may even be something to eat, if Raymond and his buddies were down there this afternoon," he added.

The two friends helped each other back down the stairs to the basement, and searched in the shadowy darkness for anything edible. Sure enough, they found a mostly eaten bag of potato chips, which they polished off in no time flat.

"Now let's go to bed," said Benjie. "I'm bushed."

"Wait," said Annie, "I think I smell something else to eat over here." She felt through the darkness with her whiskers, and her nose led her on. Soon, Annie detected the familiar smell of peanut butter.

"Oh, never mind," she said. "I've had enough peanut butter to last me a lifetime. Let's go to bed."

Benjie, who had had more to eat that day than he'd had in the past week, was quick to agree.

Chapter Seventeen

The Key

As morning light sifted through the small basement windows, Annie and Benjie came out from his sleeping place between the walls. Peering into the large room, Benjie said "What's that? I've never seen it before."

"I don't know. Let's go get a closer look," Annie replied.

They scampered across the carpet, and were soon circling warily around an odd wooden rectangle about as long as Benjie, with thin metal bars on it, and a blob of peanut butter at its edge.

"I think this is the peanut butter I almost ate last night," said Annie. "Let's eat it now. I'm hungry."

"No!" yelped Benjie.

"What's the problem?" asked Annie, her hunger making her irritable.

"I'm not sure," said the hamster slowly. "I just have a feeling that it could be dangerous.

These humans have all kinds of treacherous contraptions. I've lived here a lot longer than you have, and I know."

"Well, if you really think so," said Annie. "Anyway, I believe I heard Raymond slam the front door a little while ago. Let's go upstairs and see if we can find the spiders," she added, excited at the prospect of finally obtaining the secret key.

As they reached the small room in the hall, Annie was relieved to see that the cabinet door had been left open just enough for two little rodents to enter. With Benjie hanging nervously close behind her, she led the way to the shadowy area under the silver pipes. There, clinging to their web, were the two spiders.

"Look!" squealed Annie, not able to contain herself. "I've completed my final task, and here's my good friend Benjie to prove it!"

When the spiders merely nodded their heads in acknowledgment, Annie continued. "Since I've finished all three tasks, I was hoping you would give me the secret key — like, right now!" she said.

"The key is here, and he is yours.

He'll lead you to the out-of-doors," both spiders said together in their wispy voices.

"The outdoors! That's brilliant!" Annie

exclaimed, turning to her new friend. "We'll be free! We can get away from the Ratchets!"

Twisting back toward the spiders in confusion, she asked, "But, 'he'? Who's 'he'?"

"Um, I think they might mean me," Benjie offered.

"Huh? Well, I guess you're the only 'he' here," she said. "But how can you lead me to the out-of-doors?"

"Gosh! I've known for ages how to get outside," admitted Benjie. "But it's really scary and dangerous. I can't imagine anyone would actually want to go out there!"

"Oh, Benjie, of course we want to go out there! We'll never have to worry about the humans again!" she exulted. "And," she said to herself, "maybe I'll find my family."

"But where would we sleep? How would we get food?" Benjie blubbered.

"Silly hamster," Annie scolded, not without affection. "We'd make our own beds and find our own food. Just like we're doing already!"

"Okay. So let's say we do venture outside," said the hesitant hamster. "Where do we go from there?"

"Why, that's what a wonderful adventure is all about!" said Annie, daring to hope that her family might possibly be part of the adventure.

"We won't know until we get there, so it'll all be one great surprise!"

Benjie was slowly beginning to warm up to the idea. "I could take you downstairs now and show you the tunnel to the outside," he said. "But you'd have to positively promise to stay right by my side every minute."

"Of course. Of course," said Annie. "Let's get started! But, oh, my. I'm forgetting my manners," the little mouse added. She turned to the spiders. "Thank you so much for all your help. You've taught me an awful lot. I'll never forget you. Never!"

"Maybe we should ask them if they have any last words of advice for us," suggested Benjie.

Both spiders nodded their approval, as they climbed down their web. They descended all the way to the floor of the cabinet and stood directly in front of Annie and her new friend.

"A daisy is what you must find,

And then your owners will be kind," were the mysterious last words of the red and yellow spider.

"But . . . we don't need owners!" Annie argued. "That's why we're leaving here."

The green spider raised several of her arms above her head, in preparation for making her final pronouncement.

"Each on the other now depend,
And see the value of a friend," she whispered.

"What are you talking about? Wait!" cried Annie.

But the spiders had already turned to go, and quickly disappeared into the hole at the back of the cabinet for the last time.

Chapter Eighteen

The Tunnel

"**I** guess it's just you and me now," said Annie to her sole companion, as they made their way back downstairs.

"And we'll stay together, right?" implored Benjie, following behind.

"Yes, and we'll figure out together what the spiders meant by those last two poems," Annie added, trying to sound confident. "I guess I get the 'friend' part now, but I'm not sure I understand what they were saying about daisies and owners. Since they said our owners would be kind if we find a daisy, I think they want us to bring a daisy to Mrs. Ratchet so she'll tell Raymond to be nice to us. But I don't want to do that! I want to leave here. I want to find a new home. Don't you, Benjie? I don't know if my family would ever want to see me again, but I must have a home somewhere. I just don't know how the spiders' advice is going to get me there."

Benjie responded with a startling question.

"Annie, do you trust the spiders?"

"Well, yes I do. . . ," she admitted.

"Have they told you to do anything that was bad or that hurt you?" he pressed.

"No. The tasks they gave me were a bit strange; but they did say they'd prepare me for mortal danger."

Benjie gave a little shiver. "Oh, dear. I'd forgotten about that mortal danger," he fretted. "Do you think we'll be okay?"

"Yes, I'm sure we'll be fine," Annie assured him, "if we think calmly. We need to figure out what the spiders meant for us to do. Let's see," Annie continued. "We have to start somewhere. I believe they want you to show me the tunnel to the outside, and then we have to find a daisy when we get out there. I'm not sure what comes after that, but we can at least take those first two steps toward finding the right home for us."

"Um, by the way," asked Benjie, "what is a daisy?"

"Oh, it's a lovely white wildflower with a yellow center," Annie answered.

"There was a ferret in the pet store who had escaped from his breeders and went running around in a field one day. He told us about all kinds of beautiful-sounding flowers like black-eyed Susans and Queen Anne's lace. But he said he liked the daisies best. I can't wait to find one!"

"I guess we might as well get started," Benjie admitted. He led the way across the big room in the basement.

"You know," said Annie, as they passed the strange wooden rectangle again, "we really should eat something before we start out on our adventure. I still say we eat this peanut butter."

"Oh, Annie, please don't!" Benjie begged. "Let's see if there are any bits we might have missed in that bag we found last night." Benjie scurried over to the potato chip bag and dragged it toward Annie. As he approached, the bag bumped into the wooden rectangle. With a horrifying snap, one of its metal bars was released from its catch and came crashing down with great force right in the middle of the blob of peanut butter. "Oh, Benjie," Annie murmured. "If I hadn't listened to you. . . ." She couldn't continue.

"It's okay," he said with a little shiver. "That's what friends are for."

Completely forgetting about food for the moment, the friends gathered themselves together and proceeded on their way. Benjie continued to lead the way to the far side of the big room, to a door that Annie had not noticed before. He showed her how to squeeze under the door at its corner, and they found themselves in a dark, musty-smelling storage room. Staying close to the wall, they soon reached a small hole in the baseboard. Annie could feel the hint of a fresh breeze coming through the hole.

"This is the tunnel," announced Benjie.

He wished they could squeeze through the tunnel side by side, but it was narrow enough that they were forced to proceed in single file. Annie was a bit anxious herself, but she offered to go first, and crept straight ahead without faltering.

Soon, the fresh scent of the outdoors grew stronger. Both mouse and hamster trembled, one with excitement, and one with trepidation, as they moved faster and faster along the cramped tunnel. "Will I find my 'heart's fondest desire' outside?" Annie wondered to herself.

"I think I see light up ahead," she exclaimed from her position in the lead.

The light grew stronger, and the two friends found themselves running toward freedom as fast as their paws would carry them.

As they reached the opening into the back yard of Raymond's house, Annie stopped short. She popped out onto the grass as Benjie collided heavily with her tail end.

"Mama?" Annie squeaked.

"What?" Benjie asked, as he tumbled out behind her.

"Nothing," Annie replied in quiet disappointment, looking around at the empty back yard. She'd known in her heart that it was crazy to hope that her family would be standing out here waiting for her. "I guess our journey isn't over yet."

"Well, no, I should think it's just beginning," the hamster replied, as the two friends huddled close together, looking around them cautiously.

Chapter Nineteen

The Out-of-Doors

Annie and Benjie were crouching in a thicket of short weeds. Beyond them lay a stretch of trimmed lawn, bordered on two sides by flower gardens.

"There," piped Annie, pointing. "Maybe we can find some daisies in with all those pretty flowers."

"I don't know, Annie. Do you think it's safe to go through that short grass? Someone might see us!" Benjie sputtered. "And what about the mortal danger?"

But Annie was already scampering through the grass toward the flowering border. She was so absorbed with the sweet new smells and unusual sights of the great outdoors that the eager little mouse didn't even notice that her hamster friend was not following behind her.

"Look at all these colors!" she called over her shoulder. "Aren't they magnificent? Benjie, don't you agree?"

When there was no reply, Annie slowed, looked behind her, and finally stopped completely. Where was Benjie? From her position in the middle of the lawn, she couldn't see him still cowering in the clump of weeds near the house.

"Benjie, come on!" she called loudly.

Benjie had become so petrified with fear that his voice wouldn't work at all. All he could do was cringe in his hiding place and hope that Annie would return for him.

"Benjie!" she repeated. "Where are you? Come on!"

When there was still no reply, Annie began to feel a bit concerned. More than that, she was feeling impatient. Where was that silly hamster? Didn't he realize they had a job to do, and some serious exploration to pursue? "Why did I agree to bring him along, anyway?" she asked herself, forgetting that Benjie was the one who'd led the way to the tunnel. "I should have known I couldn't depend on him."

The green spider's last words came rushing back to Annie. "Gosh," she thought with shame, "Benjie is depending on me right now, and I'm not doing very well at seeing the value of a friend." With that, Annie went dashing back in the direction of the house. She quickly spotted the patch of weeds where they'd come out of the hole, and ran toward it as fast as her pink paws could go. Sure enough, there was poor Benjie, trembling with fright at being left alone. He broke into a broad smile as soon as he saw Annie.

Before she could utter a single word of apology, Benjie burst out, "Oh Annie, I knew you'd come back for me! You truly are a wonderful friend."

And Annie silently vowed to herself that that was exactly what she'd try to be from then on.

It took quite a little while for Annie to convince Benjie that it was safe to emerge from his hiding place.

"Why are you so afraid?" she asked. "I thought you'd been out here before."

"Well, that's just it," the skittish hamster explained. "I came out here once, and this squirrel came up to me and he was really mean and he chattered at me and threw an acorn at me and I was really scared and I ran inside and . . . and . . . I decided I'd never come back out here again," he finished.

Annie patiently explained to him that she'd already been halfway to the flower garden, and there had been nothing to be afraid of. She hadn't seen anything ahead that looked remotely dangerous. No squirrels anywhere in sight. Finally, after Annie agreed that she wouldn't forget again about her promise to stay right by Benjie's side, he consented to step out from behind the weeds and enter the grassy area.

At first he'd only creep nervously, keeping an annoyingly tight grip on Annie's tail, but soon Benjie was trotting along next to her. He let go of her tail, and the trot became a full run. Before they knew it, they'd reached the beautiful flowers.

Looking up at the blossoms from underneath, they saw all kinds of spectacular colors. They were delighted by the pinks, purples, and lavenders of all the many petals. They saw yellows and oranges and reds. But no white petals at all.

"Well," said Annie, still brimming with enthusiasm, "we'll just have to look in the garden on the other side of the lawn. I'm sure we'll find a daisy over there."

As they made their way again across the wide, grassy area, Annie was careful to stay close to Benjie, sensing that he was still a bit concerned about running in the open as they were. When they reached the garden that bordered the other side of the lawn, they repeated their careful investigation of each and every flower. After a while, even Annie admitted that the work was becoming quite tedious. When their thorough inventory finally came to an end, they'd still not discovered a single white flower.

"It's okay," she said to Benjie, trying to mask her disappointment. "We'll have to go farther and look harder. We'll probably have to go beyond this yard to find what we're looking for."

With Benjie at her side, Annie set off with determination toward the back of the yard. They halted, as they found themselves looking straight up at a tall, metal barrier.

Chapter Twenty

The Broom

"This won't stop us," said Annie, scowling at the chain link fence. "We can fit right through those holes." Before either could move forward, however, they were stopped in their tracks by a frightful yowl.

"Go, Benjie, through the holes!" Annie yelled, looking over her shoulder at the neighbor's cat. Lucifer was on the far side of the Ratchet's backyard, but he was bearing down on them quickly. Mouse and hamster scrambled through the fence, and turned in time to see the hissing cat stop short before the barrier. They held onto each other and watched in terror as Lucifer began to carefully climb the fence.

Benjie pulled at Annie's hand. "Come on, Annie! We have to go!" he cried.

"No, Benjie. We can't outrun that cat. We've got to think of something else," she said frantically.

With a startling crash, their former nemesis

came storming through the back door with her infamous broom. "Drat you, Lucifer!" Raymond's mother yelled. "How many times have I told you to stay on your own property!" she scolded, charging at the cat and wildly swinging her broom.

With one last baleful look at the two terrified rodents, Lucifer leaped off the fence, and streaked away toward his own back yard, expertly dodging the flailing broom.

"And stay out!" Mrs. Ratchet shouted after him, slamming the back door behind her.

"Okay — now we run," said Annie, wanting to put as much distance as possible between them and the cat, in case he decided to attempt any further pursuit.

Running until they could run no more, the friends finally flopped to the ground in exhaustion, and found themselves in a lovely meadow. They gazed, through the fading light, out on rolling fields of low grasses, which were strewn here and there with beautiful, subtly colored clumps of wildflowers in every direction.

"Let's get going," cried Annie. "Look at all those flowers! There must be a daisy here some place."

"But, Annie, it's getting dark. And I'm hungry, and I'm tired, and I'm scared! And what if that cat finds us!" wailed Benjie. "Can't we go back in the house?"

"Oh, no, sir!" Annie chided. "We will never go back there. But I do agree that it's time we started looking for dinner and a place to spend the night."

Hurrying through the failing daylight, the two friends quickly came upon a large thicket of raspberry bushes. They filled themselves with the luscious fruit, realizing that neither of them had had a bite to eat since the day before. Then they went about the task of securing a place to sleep.

They stepped cautiously out into the open field, but soon realized that there was no other adequate place for them to take cover in the wide-open expanse. Shortly, they found their way back to the raspberry thicket. It was awfully prickly under the thorny branches, but, since there seemed to be no alternative, hamster and mouse both tried to settle down and sleep.

Annie lay awake for quite a while, trying to ignore the scratchy branches that nudged her every time the wind swayed the boughs of the raspberry bush. She thought that Benjie had fallen fast asleep, when he sat up and asked in a frightened voice, "What was that?"

"I don't know, Benjie. What did you hear?"

she asked.

"That! That rustling sound. Don't you hear it? What is that?" he implored.

Annie shook herself into alertness and listened intently. Sure enough, she did hear a faint rustling sound not too far from their makeshift bedroom. She carefully crept to the edge of the thicket and peered out into the moonlit meadow. Several feet in front of her, and pawing through the grass, she saw a sleek brown ferret.

Chapter Twenty-One

The Ferret

"Franky, is that you?" Annie called cautiously.

"What? Who's that?" blurted the ferret, snapping his head up.

"It's me, Annie. From Mr. Dailey's pet store. Do you remember me?" she asked.

"Oh, yeah! Annie! How you doin'?" Franky replied, heading toward the raspberry bush. "What you doin' out here in the big wide world? And who, may I inquire, is this?" he asked, spying Benjie cowering next to his friend.

"Oh, well, it's a long story, but the short version is, this is my friend Benjie, and we're on an adventure," Annie replied. "And what are you doing out here?" she asked.

"I got out — again! You know us ferrets. We just ain't made for the indoor life," Franky said with a chuckle.

"Yes, I love this being outdoors!" Annie exulted. "The air is so fresh, and it all seems so wild and free."

"Yeah, well, speakin' of . . . you two little guys need to be real careful out here. I ain't sure it's such a good idea for a couple of pet-store rodents to be out and about when you don't know the ropes, so to speak," the ferret added with concern.

"But we must!" said Benjie, surprising them all. "We're on a mission. It's . . . well, we don't really know what it is, but it's important. We need to be here," he said with conviction.

"Well, alrighty, then. Good for you, little guy," said the impressed ferret. "Maybe just let me give you a couple pointers, okay?"

Both hamster and mouse nodded their heads in assent. They'd need all the help they could get out here.

"So, first," began Franky, "you gotta stay under cover at night. This bush is a good spot. Now, it would be best to stay undercover all day, too, but then you wouldn't get nowhere, I can see that. So, you're gonna have to stay low an' move fast to get through this meadow."

The rodents listened intently. They both pricked up their ears at the ferret's last bit of advice.

"And," he finished, "you gotta look out for the mortal danger!"

"Oh, yes, we've been warned about that already," Annie squeaked.

"B . . . but, what is it?" Benjie implored.

"I don't honestly know for sure," Franky admitted. "I ain't never met one, myself. But I do know that they swoop down from the sky, and you gotta be on the lookout all the time," he ended, staring sternly at his listeners.

"Gosh, Annie," Benjie faltered. "I don't know, now. Do you think we should go back to the house in the morning?"

"Now, what did you just say a minute ago?" Annie asked her friend. "Didn't you just say we're on an important mission? We can do this together, right?"

"Right! Okay — we can do this together. Friends to the end," agreed Benjie, his conviction restored by Annie's brave words.

Despite her bravado, Annie herself was feeling quite apprehensive about the possibility of encountering the mortal danger. "Um, any chance you could stay with us and guide us through the meadow in the morning?" she asked Franky.

"Sorry. No can do, little gal. I got myself a family now, over in the next meadow. I should be gettin' back to them directly. You guys listen to my advice and you'll be fine," he said, backing out of the thicket. "Just stay on the lookout. . . ." Franky's words faded away as he disappeared into the night.

"Oh, okay . . . 'bye . . . and thanks!" Annie waved, calling into the moonlight.

With that, the two weary rodents looked worriedly into each other's eyes and settled down for a long night of wakeful thoughts and fitful sleep.

Chapter Twenty-Two

The Meadow

For the first time in their lives, Annie and Benjie were awakened by the sun's morning light. They watched in wonder as the sky slowly lit with more colors than they'd seen in the flower garden. Hamster and mouse stood in silent awe, having no words for the scene that played in the skies above them. When nothing was left in the sky but a pure, cloudless blue, they finally lowered their eyes and stared at each other.

"Well, we have work to do, don't we?" said Annie, trying not to think too much about Franky's warning words.

Benjie could only nod in agreement, his mind similarly occupied.

"No sense setting out on an empty stomach," said Annie, all business. They both refueled on as many raspberries as they could handle, and headed purposefully toward the nearest clump of wildflowers.

"Remember to stay low and move fast,"

Annie reminded her friend.

"And keep watching the sky for the mortal danger, right?" Benjie squeaked.

"Yes, right," Annie agreed. "I'm sure we'll be fine," she added, for her friend's benefit as well as her own.

As they closed in on a tall bunch of blossoms, Benjie began jumping up and down excitedly, momentarily forgetting the directive to stay low.

"Look, Annie, look!" he cried. "I see white petals!"

They both took off at a fast clip and arrived out of breath under the white flowers at the same time.

"I can't tell if they have yellow centers from down here," Annie observed. "I'm going to try to climb up a stem and see."

"Oh, I don't know . . . do you think that's safe?" asked Benjie.

"Sure, you just watch the sky while I'm climbing up, okay?"

"Yes . . . okay," the nervous hamster agreed, quickly raising his gaze to the clouds.

Annie shimmied up the thin stalk. When she was just over halfway up, the stem began to buckle under her weight.

"Whoa!" she yelled, and, "Wheee!" as the flower stem bent over double and gently lowered her to the ground. As Annie hopped down from the stem, she noticed a look of disappointment on Benjie's face.

"I'm sorry. No yellow center," he said.

"Oh, you're right," agreed Annie. "In fact, this looks a lot like the white Queen Anne's lace Franky told me about in the pet store. It's all right," she added. "There are lots and lots of flowers in this meadow. I'm sure we'll find some daisies very soon."

Annie didn't add that, once they found them, she had no idea what their next step would be.

The determined little rodents spent the rest of the morning and most of the afternoon traveling from one bunch of wildflowers to the next, in search of daisies. They ranged all over that broad meadow, finding black-eyed Susans, devil's paintbrush, and buttercups, but not a single daisy.

Chapter Twenty-Three

The Mortal Danger

When the sun was at its hottest in the mid-afternoon, the industrious little explorers decided to take a break. Annie and Benjie both lay down in the grass and stared up at the blue expanse of sky. They found themselves scanning carefully for anything that might turn into a mortal danger, as they fanned themselves with bits of leaves that had blown into the field from a nearby stand of trees. Soon, Benjie was snoring softly, exhausted by their non-stop activity.

Forcing herself to stay alert, Annie's sharp eye caught a dark shape circling far above. She didn't know what it was, but a primitive instinct rose up from deep inside her, warning her that this was the mortal danger they'd been fearing.

"Quick!" she said urgently. "We've got to hide."

As Benjie wakened groggily from his afternoon nap, Annie looked up at the menacing shape circling lower. "Think, Annie, think," she commanded herself. In a flash, the thought of hiding under her sock-bed came to her.

A gentle breeze sent a couple of leaves tumbling by them. "That's it!" squeaked Annie, and she pounced on the leaves before they could pass by.

"What's going on?" asked the confused and sleepy hamster.

"Get under this leaf and don't make a sound!" whispered Annie.

Thinking this was all some new sort of game, Benjie obeyed happily. But his smile turned to a look of sheer terror as the bloodcurdling screech of a hawk split the air above them.

"Just don't move. Just don't breathe," Annie willed silently. Benjie had no choice but to unknowingly comply, being completely frozen with fear.

Annie dared not peek out from under her leaf disguise, but she could hear the hawk's menacing calls coming nearer. Soon, it was so close that she could hear the swoosh of its wings, swooping down toward their flimsy hiding places.

As she was thinking that all hope was lost, Annie heard an angry hissing, and a rapid flapping sound, followed by a triumphant squawk. Unable to stop herself from looking now,

Annie peered around the edge of her leaf and saw the mortal danger ascending into the sky with a small snake in its claws.

An eternity seemed to pass before the hawk's cries faded into the distance and finally disappeared altogether. When she was fairly sure it was safe, Annie stole a glance from under her leaf again. She rolled over and nudged Benjie.

"Are you okay, my friend?" she asked.

"Was that the mortal danger, Annie?" he gulped.

"Yes. Yes, it was the mortal danger," she said. "And we're all right!" Annie realized as she said it.

"But it could come back, couldn't it?" Benjie almost hated to ask.

"Yes, you're right," she agreed. "We'd better keep these leaves on top of us and head for those trees over there."

By the time they reached the edge of the forest, the sun was preparing to set. As Benjie flopped down in an exhausted heap, Annie went in search of dinner. They ate one acorn apiece, and fell into a deep sleep under their leaf blankets.

Chapter Twenty-Four

The Forest

Both mouse and hamster awoke to the gentle sounds of dawn in the forest. Little birds chirped, leaves rustled, and Annie heard a splashing sound in the distance that she couldn't quite identify.

After a hearty breakfast of wild blueberries and more acorns, the two companions set out again on their quest for the elusive daisy. They shuffled through the spent leaves and prickly pine needles on the forest floor, systematically moving from tree to tree. Here and there they did come across some deliciously fragrant primroses, and delicate indigo violets, but by noon they both were beginning to doubt that they'd ever find the white-petaled, yellow-centered daisy.

"Let's take a lunch break," suggested Benjie.

"Great idea," agreed Annie. As they roamed deeper into the forest, foraging for nuts and berries, the splashing sound Annie had heard earlier grew louder and more distinct. As they crested a small hillock, both friends stopped in wonder, Benjie nearly dropping his armful of goodies. There before them ran a slowly meandering stream, with circling eddies of leaf debris, stretching into the distance in both directions as far as either of them could see.

"Let's have our picnic here," suggested Benjie. "This is a lovely view!"

They found a mossy spot on a slab of rock overlooking the stream, and settled down to enjoy their lunch and the scenery. As they brushed the last crumbs of lunch from their whiskers, Annie stood up. "Benjie," she said, "we've got to figure out a way to get to the other side of this water."

"Sure," said Benjie. "I know how to swim. All rodents do," he called back over his shoulder as he ran toward the stream's edge.

"No, Benjie, no!" cried Annie, racing to his side. "This water is moving around too much. It would sweep us away and take us under! Just like the blue water under the seat in the spiders' room. We'll have to think of a way to get across the water without going into it," she added, remembering her solution to crossing the blue whirlpool. "I'm sure we can find something here in the forest that will stretch across the stream."

Annie and Benjie both surveyed the

surrounding area, looking for something solid to bridge the spiraling current.

"How about this?" offered the hamster, pushing at a middle-sized rock.

"I'm afraid that wouldn't go all the way across," Annie counseled.

"How's this?" he asked, this time pulling at a long, thin tree branch.

"Perfect!" Annie exclaimed. "It looks long enough to go across, and just wide enough for us to walk on. Good work, Benjie," she praised, as he swelled with pride.

"Here, I'll take it," Annie said, as she wrestled the end of the branch away from Benjie. The little mouse began tugging with all her might, trying to drag the tree limb to the water's edge on her own. It was much heavier than she'd expected.

"Annie, let me help you," Benjie offered.

"I've got it, I've got it!" she insisted, reverting to her old ways of stubborn independence.

"Annie, we've been through this before," Benjie spoke up. "Remember the value of a friend — we do things together, right? Come on. You take that end and I'll grab this one."

"I guess you're right," Annie relented with a smile, and, working as a team, the two friends were able to shift the stick down to the edge of the stream. With Annie steadying the front end and Benjie shoving from behind, they maneuvered the branch across the short expanse of water until the far end rested on the other side.

The mouse made the treacherous crossing first, while the hamster held the limb as stable as possible by clamping it with his little paws. When Annie arrived safely on the far shore, she gave a little wave of thanks and triumph. Benjie pushed his end of the stick into the mud as far as he could force it to go, and Annie held her end of the branch as tightly as possible so Benjie could begin his careful crawl across.

When Benjie was just halfway across, the branch shifted in the water. Benjie and Annie watched in horror as its larger end was pulled out of the mud with a sickening sucking sound. Benjie and the stick started moving downstream, and Annie was dragged roughly through the mud and quickly toward the edge of the water, as she refused to relinquish her hold on the branch.

"Annie, let go — now!" Benjie screamed, and Annie was too terrified to do anything else. She leaped back and watched in disbelief as Benjie and the branch moved inexorably away from her, through slowly rotating clumps of floating leaves and pine needles.

Chapter Twenty-Five

The Parting

Annie ran along the shore, shouting, "Hold on Benjie. I'll save you!" all the while wondering what in the world she could do to help her friend. The sound of the water grew louder as both mouse and hamster moved downstream. Annie looked ahead of her, searching for the source of the ever-louder crashing sound, and halted momentarily in amazement at the majestic and harrowing sight of a small waterfall up ahead. It might have been small as waterfalls go, but, to these tiny rodents, it looked like Niagara Falls.

"Oh, how did we come to be in this predicament?" Annie asked herself in anguish. If she had to be abandoned by Mr. Dailey and her parents, at least they could have given her to someone nicer, who would have fed her and cared for her. "It's all the fault of that awful boy Raymond Ratchet. Right?" she questioned. "I don't know," she thought distractedly. "I'd better think about saving Benjie now, and ask questions later."

Annie realized that Benjie was moving more and more rapidly downstream, and she was certain that it would be very dangerous for Benjie and his branch to make contact with that gushing mountain of waterfall. "Think, Annie, think!" she said to herself, as she careened along the shoreline, trying to keep pace with her floating friend. She quickly realized that the branch was spiraling through the water very close to the shore on the other side of the stream.

"Benjie, you're going to have to jump to shore!" she yelled, over the rushing roar of the water.

"I can't move. I'm too scared!" he screamed back.

"Yes you can. You have to. Now — go NOW!" Annie commanded. Across the water, Benjie locked eyes with his dear friend, gathered all of his courage, and turned to give a mighty leap toward shore. He landed in the mud just at the water's edge and lay in an immobile heap, as the branch he'd been riding crashed through the waterfall and disappeared under the dark water.

"Benjie, you did it! Get up! You're okay! Right?" Annie shouted. Benjie lifted his little head, and gave a shaky wave to Annie across the stream. "Oh, Annie, I could never have done it without you! Why, you've saved my life over and over again. And I'd still be back in that shadowy basement if not for you. You're my hero! You've been. . . ."

"Wait Benjie," Annie cut in, calling across the water. "We've been working as a team all along," she realized out loud. "You saved my life, too, you know, when you warned me about the peanut butter in the basement. And I'd still be looking for a way out of the house, if not for you! So, you see, we're each other's heroes!"

"So . . . what are we heroes supposed to do now?" Benjie cried.

It dawned on them both at the same moment that they were on opposite sides of the stream, with no known way to cross safely to each other.

"Annie, you . . . you'll have to go on without me," Benjie squeaked.

"What?" called his best friend.

"You have to go on alone!" the little hamster yelled, his strength rising up.

"Oh, no, Benjie. . . ," Annie began.

"Yes!" Benjie declared with all his courage. "You must go on and find the daisy. I'm going to be fine."

"But what will you do? Where will you go?" Annie wailed.

"I'm . . . I'm going to find my own adventure,"

he asserted. "I'm a brave hamster now. I'm going to go have a brave hamster adventure."

"Yes, yes, you are," agreed Annie. "And I'm going to go find my daisy, and we're both going to be okay," she called. "But I'm really going to miss you!"

What more could these two dear friends possibly say to each other as their parting drew so quickly near? Having emptied their hearts after their treacherous adventure, they each found only three more words necessary.

"I love you," shouted Benjie, ending with a little sob.

"I love you," Annie called, with as much bravery as she could muster.

Both hamster and mouse pried their eyes away from each other and set off with determination in their divergent directions.

Having traveled only about ten feet into the forest, Annie couldn't help but turn and look back. There was Benjie, just a few yards up the stream, looking longingly back at her. Annie forced herself to give a cheerful wave and headed northward once more. She didn't stop until the rushing sound of the waterfall had faded into the distance.

Chapter Twenty-Six

The Daisy

Annie plodded straight ahead through the woods all afternoon, not even stopping to investigate the occasional clumps of wildflowers she spied. The little mouse felt strangely sure that she would not find a daisy until after she'd left the forest.

As she trudged along alone, Annie had time to contemplate the difficult questions she'd posed to herself earlier. Was there blame to be cast here, for this whole challenging situation? If so, did it land squarely on the shoulders of Raymond Ratchet? "Perhaps. Perhaps not," she admitted honestly. Was it not more useful to spend her time thinking about what lessons she was learning through the challenges she faced, rather than determining who was responsible for those challenges? "Yes, absolutely!" Annie decided, and she spent the rest of the afternoon pondering all the good and important things she'd learned over the past weeks. Most importantly, she'd learned that sometimes it's good to be independent, and sometimes it's even better to work together.

At last, as the sun was just beginning to think about heading toward the west, the weary little mouse climbed up a gentle rise, and there, stretching before her, was a glorious open field. At first, Annie feared that this might be the same meadow that she and Benjie had traversed the day before, but she realized with relief that it couldn't be, since she'd not again come upon the stream in her travels.

Before emerging from the safety of the forest, Annie had the presence of mind to pick up a leaf from the forest floor. She could use this to hide beneath, just in case she again encountered any mortal danger.

As she peered out through the brush at the edge of the woods, Annie saw a lovely, white farm house, and she found herself drawn to it, as she walked bravely in that direction. Although she realized that humans were likely to be in or around such a structure, she couldn't seem to fight the impulse to approach the house. As Annie drew nearer, she heard the sound of voices, and soon she spied two humans sitting on a wide covered porch. She quickly concealed herself under her leaf disguise, and stealthily continued her approach.

Presently, the larger of the two humans, who both seemed to be females, entered the dwelling. The smaller female hopped off the porch and plopped down onto the grass, not three yards from where Annie was hiding.

Annie peeked ever so carefully out from the edge of the leaf, and found herself staring at the most beautiful little girl she'd ever seen. Annie had seen lots of girls come into the pet store before she'd been taken away by Raymond, but none of them had seemed as purely lovely as this one. This child had shiny dark hair, which cascaded around her shoulders in glossy curls. She had rosy, round cheeks in a coffee-and-cream complexion, and a happy, contented smile. And, most remarkably, she had eyes the exact same shade of blue as Annie's!

Annie was startled from her reverie by the sound of a screen door opening. The larger human, the child's mother, came back out onto the porch and leaned over the railing.

"Daisy," she called gently, "it's almost time to come in and set the table for supper. You can have five more minutes to play."

"Daisy?" said Annie to herself in disbelief. "Is this my Daisy? Could it be? Why, she's not a flower at all!" And without another thought, Annie threw off her leaf covering and scampered straight toward the little girl.

Daisy saw Annie immediately, and knelt down to get a closer look at her. The girl placed her open palm on the grass as Annie approached, and the little mouse climbed right up onto her hand.

As Daisy lifted Annie up toward her face, she said quietly, "Oh, aren't you a pretty thing? I've never seen a mouse with blue eyes before. Come on inside so you can meet my mama."

"Look, Mama," Daisy said with delight, bringing Annie into the farmhouse. "I found this dear little mouse out on the lawn. Do you think she'd like to play with Sunshine?"

"Oh, I don't know, darling," Daisy's mother cautioned. "Field mice don't always get along with pet store mice."

"But I think this is a pet store mouse," Daisy explained. "And a very special one. Look at her blue eyes!"

"Gracious! She does look special," exclaimed Daisy's mother. "And not like any field mouse I've ever seen. In fact, I think I remember your Uncle Bob telling us about an unusual blue-eyed mouse at his pet store. Why don't you go on up and introduce her to Sunshine?"

With that, Daisy was bounding up the farmhouse stairs, cradling Annie safely against her chest. Annie looked around her curiously as they entered the child's bedroom. There was a single bed with a simple, white bedspread, and a dark, wooden dresser that gleamed with careful polishing. The walls were papered with a delicate pattern of blue ribbons and daisies — the floral kind. And, on a small table, there rested a shiny, metal cage lined with fragrant pine shavings. Annie's ears pricked up as she spied the tiny mouse inside.

Chapter Twenty-Seven

The Reunion

"Sunshine, I've found a new friend for you," Daisy said, and she lowered Annie to where she could look into the cage.

Annie shook her whiskers in disbelief. "Ethel?" she said. "Is that you?"

"Annie? My big sister, Annie! Can it be true?" squeaked the tiny Ethel. "How ever did you get here? We thought you were gone from us forever!"

Since the two mice seemed to be communicating in a friendly way, Daisy opened the little hinged door to the cage and placed Annie inside. The sisters hugged and danced and squealed with delight. Daisy was happy to see them getting along so well. When she was sure that it was quite all right to leave them alone together, the little girl went off downstairs to help her mother with preparations for supper.

Annie's delight at seeing her sister was tempered by the remembrance that her family had allowed her to be taken away. Apparently, they'd not cared enough to keep Ethel, either. She'd have to pose her questions about their family carefully.

"Ethel," she began, "aren't you sad that Mama and Papa gave you away, too?"

"Oh, no, Annie!" her sister cried in dismay. "They didn't give us away! They had no choice! We were all very sad after you left, but we tried to tell ourselves that you were going to have a better life with a human family."

"Really?" asked Annie with a tearful smile.

"Of course!" Ethel replied. "While I was still at the pet store, we talked about you every day and wished you well, and remembered you in our prayers every night. And now I'm sure they're thinking of both of us, as I get to be with a wonderful human family, too."

"Well, actually," Annie admitted, "it wasn't so wonderful at Raymond Ratchet's house. It was so bad, in fact, that I had to run away, and that's how I came to be in the field outside your new house."

"Oh, my poor Annie," said Ethel, her eyes wide. "You must tell me all about it!"

Ethel was amazed by her big sister's tales of danger and adventure as well as friendship. She asked Annie to tell her again and again about how she'd brought the beautiful pink cupcakes all the way down the stairs to Benjie the hamster. Annie couldn't help feeling sad as she spoke about Benjie, realizing that she was not likely to ever see him again.

Annie's little sister was horrified to hear of Raymond's neglectful treatment. "Daisy isn't like that at all," Ethel told her sister with confidence. "She came into Mr. Dailey's store and brought me here not long after Raymond took you away, and she takes me out of the cage and pets me and plays with me every day. She's very careful to keep my shavings clean and my seed bowl and water bottle filled. I know you'll just love living here with Daisy and me."

"That sounds very nice," said Annie. "Though it surely would be great to be back at the pet store with the rest of the family. Don't you think?"

"Why, Annie, that's the best part," Ethel crowed. "Daisy's full name is Daisy Dailey, and her Uncle Bob is our Mr. Dailey from the pet store! She's already taken me back to the store a few times to visit with the family, and she promised to take me as often as I like!"

To make things even more wonderful, Daisy came back upstairs after supper to tell the mice that her parents had agreed to allow Annie to live with them. She took them both out of the cage and, holding one in each hand, gave Annie a tour of the whole farmhouse. Daisy walked slowly, touring each of the orderly and well-cared-for rooms of the old house. Annie was introduced to Daisy's daddy, who was Mr. Dailey's brother. He was very friendly and gave both mice a ride on his knee. Daisy's mama also held each of the mice for a few moments, tickling their whiskers with her nose in a motherly way.

As the two mouse sisters snuggled down together into clean pine shavings that night, Annie was brimming with happy thoughts. Being able to live here with Ethel and Daisy would be so lovely, and the possibility of visiting with her family whenever she liked was a dream come true.

Because they'd brought her to this wonderful place, all the difficult and frightening experiences she'd had since first leaving her family now seemed quite worthwhile.

Annie's only regret was her uncertainty about Benjie's whereabouts. She turned toward her sleepy sister. "Ethel, did you say you were all praying for me at bedtime each night?"

"Huh? Oh, yes," the younger mouse murmured. "You know Mama taught us all to do that," she said with a yawn.

"I think those prayers really helped me," Annie continued. "There were so many situations where Benjie and I were in danger, and we escaped each time. I think we should pray for Benjie, to make sure he'll stay safe too."

"That's nice. . . ," said Ethel, in a snoozy squeak, as she turned over onto her side.

Annie knew she had some thoughtful work to do before she could drift off to sleep too. She set about praying that her dear friend would find his way to a wonderful home, just as she had. She didn't go to sleep until she was sure of it.

Chapter Twenty-Eight

The Homecoming

The next morning, Daisy's mother suggested that they take Sunshine and Annie (now being called Raindrop) to Uncle Bob's pet store that afternoon, to see if he could give them a clue as to where the new mouse had come from. Annie was beside herself with anticipation, as she and Ethel were gently placed in a covered shoebox for their trip to the pet store.

"Won't Mama and Papa and all the others be surprised?" squeaked Ethel. Annie was so excited she could hardly reply.

When they arrived at Dailey's Pet Emporium, Daisy carefully carried the shoebox into the store and placed it gingerly on the counter. "Come see what we have here, Uncle Bob," she called, as she lifted the lid.

"Well, I'll be!" said Mr. Dailey, scooping Annie into his hand. "I thought you were living with that Raymond Ratchet! I've been regretting selling you to him ever since," he said to Annie, as he stroked her head.

Uncle Bob listened thoughtfully, as Daisy explained how she'd found Annie in the farmyard the day before.

"This clever little critter must have had herself quite an adventure, traveling all the way from the Ratchet's neighborhood to the farmhouse. I wonder how she knew the way to where her sister is living. I guess we'll never know. That is, unless you'd care to tell us, little mouse," he said with a wink and a grin.

Annie was lowered gently back into the box, and Daisy carried it over to where the whole mouse family was waiting excitedly. They'd seen Daisy come in, so they knew they'd be having a visit from Ethel, but imagine their surprise when Annie was handed down into their glass case right behind her younger sister! There were squeals and hugs all around and lots of dancing.

"Oh, Mama!" Annie cried. "I missed you so much, and I thought I'd never see you again," she said through her tears. Having grown up a good bit over the last few weeks, the oldest mouse sister realized that it would be kinder not to tell her family how she'd thought they'd abandoned her. Their hugs and loving words were all that she needed to put those thoughts to rest for good.

Then there were some very special introductions. Since Ethel's last visit, Mrs. Mouse had delivered a whole new litter of brothers and sisters. They were named Fanny, Garry, Harry, Izzy and Joel. They were so new that they looked more pink than white, and Annie and Ethel delighted in petting and cooing over them.

After all the flurry had settled down, Annie agreed to retell the amazing story of her adventures since she'd left the pet store. Mother and Father mouse and all the siblings, from Barry to Joel, sat with their mouths hanging open, though this was more due to hunger than fascination, on the part of the youngest five.

Chapter Twenty-Nine

The Farewells

As Annie was just getting to the part in her story where she'd spied the beautiful farmhouse from the edge of the woods, she stopped short. She couldn't believe her ears. Was that Raymond Ratchet's unpleasant voice she was hearing? Sure enough, there he was, stomping toward their glass case.

"Since that stupid mouse ran away," he was saying over his shoulder, "I'm going to find a new pet. Maybe another mouse, even."

Raymond stopped right in front of the mouse family's home. "Say! That's my mouse. I know he's the only one with blue eyes. What's he doing back here?" As Raymond pressed his nose to the glass and glared at Annie, Mr. Dailey came up behind him.

"Can I help you with something, Raymond?" he asked.

"Yeah, you can give me back my mouse. I paid good money for him, and I want him back.

He's mine!"

"Raymond, I have to tell you that I think I made a mistake when I sold that particular mouse to you. I sold her to you for three dollars, if I recall correctly, but I believe that she's actually worth more than that."

"Say, what are you trying to pull?" the boy demanded.

"Raymond, I would very much like to buy that mouse back from you. I'm willing to pay you according to her actual worth, which I believe is ten dollars. Would you be willing to agree to that?" inquired Mr. Dailey.

"Are you kidding? Sure! Can you give me the money right now?" asked Raymond with a greedy grin. "Hey!" he hollered to his friend Zach farther down the same aisle. "This will be enough money to get that video game I've been wanting. Forget about a stupid pet!"

While Raymond was busy collecting his money from the cash register up front, Annie noticed that Zach was coming down the aisle toward the rodent cases. He was carefully examining the shelves that held hamster food and equipment.

"Let's see," Zach was saying. "We'll need food, and a wheel, and some pine shavings. What else, Buddy?" As he spoke, he slowly withdrew something from his pocket, and held it up near the shelf of hamster supplies.

Annie was sure she must be mistaken, but the fuzzy ball in Zach's hand looked an awful lot like Benjie.

"Here, Buddy," Zach said in a low, calm voice. "Let me put you down for a minute, so I can read this package. Would you like to come over here and look at these cute mice?"

"Annie, is that you?" squeaked a familiar voice, as Benjie was handed gently onto the shelf next to the mouse case.

"Benjie!" cried Annie. "How did you get here? What are you doing with Zach? I'm so happy to see you!" she blurted.

Benjie explained that, after he'd parted from Annie at the stream, he'd hiked until almost dark and then spent a chilly night in the woods. He'd forged ahead the next morning, feeling revived and inspired. As he'd neared the edge of the woods, he met Zach, who lived in a nice house in a clearing nearby. Zach had taken him inside and made a temporary home for him in a laundry basket. Since Zach's mother had said that he could keep Benjie, they were here now to pick out some proper pet supplies.

A cloud crossed Annie's face as she thought of something terrible. "Benjie," she whispered, "has Raymond seen you with Zach? He was just trying to get Mr. Dailey to give me back to him, and he might want you back, too!" she croaked in horror.

"Oh, no, no," Benjie assured her. "Raymond did see me at Zach's house, and he just asked Zach why he wanted such a ratty old rodent, and then ignored me. I think it'd been such a long time since he'd bought me that he didn't even recognize me. Zach is so nice to me, though," Benjie added with a contented sigh. "He calls me Buddy and he says I'm his new best friend! And what about you, Annie?"

Annie filled Benjie in on all that had happened to her since their parting in the forest. He was amazed to hear that Daisy was not a flower after all, but a lovely little girl. They laughed and talked together about their shared adventures, and both expressed their gratitude that they'd had the courage to go on after they became separated in the woods.

As they were saying their farewells, Benjie was carefully scooped up and placed back in Zach's warm pocket. Annie felt happy and sad at the same time as she waved goodbye.

It was time to say goodbye to Mama and Papa and the mouse brothers and sisters. This was not at all hard to do, since Annie knew she could come back any time. And besides, she'd have her sister Ethel, and her new owner, Daisy, with her every day in her wonderful new life at the farmhouse.

Annie and Ethel were quiet in the shoebox as they rode home in the car on Daisy's lap. Ethel was fast asleep, and Annie was remembering. She recalled the spiders, and how much they'd helped her. She thought about Benjie, and what a good friend he'd become. Her heart swelled with gratitude for her family and Daisy. With a shiver, her thoughts glanced over her frightening experiences with the Ratchets, the mortal danger, and the waterfall. But, as she was drifting off toward sleep, lulled by the motion of the car, these unpleasant thoughts seemed to fade into a distant shadowy past. Annie was sure that more happy adventures were just around the corner. But first, she'd better get some rest . . . and maybe a snack!

36405661R00078

Made in the USA
Charleston, SC
01 December 2014